Frank "

1948

The year the countdown to Armageddon began

To Renee,

Best Always,

Ray Antonuco (aka "Zook")

Copyright Publishing

As a complete work of fiction by Create Space, a division of Amazon, Inc.

Copyright first edition@2015

Printed in the USA at Charleston, South Carolina

Authored by Frank "Zook" Lo Zucco

ISBN9781505326222

Library of Congress in publication data processing

i

Major Endorsements: What Some Christian Leaders Are Saying About *1948*

"Our world is filled with wars, nuclear weapons, terrorism and beheadings, poverty, financial collapse, and death delivering Ebola. Any one of these could bring about the end of the world as we know it. *1948* is a fictional work that you will enjoy and that will make you think. This book is a cross-over, because it explores both secular and Christian mind-sets. It is a must read for the open-minded!"

Dr. Cornell "Corkie" Haan

Kingdom Connections

Mission America Coalition

Cave Creek, AZ

"The author of the fictional work *1948* gradually draws the reader into a perspective of global events that he believes will inevitably lead to a third world conflict. The countdown for this conflict, the author posits, actually began in the year *1948*. In the process, *1948* goes well beyond George Orwell's *1984*, in predictions and discussions of world events. Enjoyable and interesting, *1948* is engaging reading for the believer or skeptic."

Gary W. Passero

National Vice President

Business Men's Fellowship of America

"All readers, whatever their world views, will find much to stimulate their thinking and emotions in this book. *1948* also provides coverage of a number of important geo-political and religious issues of today. This is a must read for those who are willing to attempt to interpret political events today in the light of historical claims."

William J Stauff MBA DST

Administrative faculty in higher education at Harvard University and The University of Georgia.

"*1948,* although a fictional story, invites the reader into the private world of two couples who, through God's Providence, have formed a wonderfully close bond of friendship. This, despite the fact that one couple is seriously Christian and their friends are secular Jews. The story takes the reader on a roller coaster ride ranging from the meeting of interesting "key players," to the excitement of a journey to Israel (with a treasure trove of great information) and concluding with an event that left me wanting me to read on…and fast. *1948* is an effective tool to share the "reason for the hope that is within us." As a true to life story, *1948* is also riveting. I would highly recommend *1948* to any who have a heart to share their faith with family, friends and their personal "Jerusalem."

Wayne Taylor

General Manager

Mars Hill Christian Radio Network of New York and Canada

Disclaimer

This book is sold for the primary purpose of provoking thought and enjoyment. It is a work of fiction. Names, locales, characters, events and incidents are the product of the author's imagination and/or are used fictitiously as to its characters and their exploits. Thus neither the author nor the publisher will be held accountable for the use of information contained in this book as to any resemblance to any actual, business, company, event, locale or person, living or dead.

Author

A veteran educator, the author is also a professional freelance writer in newspapers and magazines, a school consultant and an emerging leader in the field of anti-bullying. He holds undergraduate degrees in history, theology and education, as well as masters and doctoral degrees in educational leadership. *1948* is his first published book in addition to his doctoral dissertation. Like George Orwell of *1984* fame, he has chosen to write under a pen name.

Dedication

To my supportive wife Elaine, who patiently put up with this impatient author.

Special Appreciation

The author, from New York, is especially grateful to Brian and Edie Johnson for hosting him in their Virgin Island home during his final proof review of this book. Like some authors of old, who were inspired by the tropics to turn out works such as Treasure Island and Robinson Crusoe, the author was also able to be inspired, while at the same time working in complete peace, solitude and warmth during January, 2015.

1948

The year the countdown to Armageddon began

Table of Contents

Major Endorsements   **ii**

Disclaimer   **iv**

Author   **v**

Dedication   **vi**

CHAPTER 1   **1**

WHAT'S IN A NAME?

CHAPTER 2   **5**

A CHANGING OF THE GUARD

CHAPTER 3   **9**

PROFESSOR AL

CHAPTER 4   **18**

MENTOR AL

CHAPTER 5   ☐☐

    OLD FRIENDS REUNITE

CHAPTER 6   ☐9

    CATCHING UP

CHAPTER 7   ☐9

    DINNER AT THE MORETTIS

CHAPTER 8   5☐

    JOE'S LETTER

CHAPTER 9   5☐

    DINNER AT THE STEINS

CHAPTER 10   ☐1

    GIRLS' NIGHT OUT

CHAPTER 11   ☐9

    ISRAEL ANYONE?

CHAPTER 12   89

    THE MORETTIS' BIG DECISION

CHAPTER 13   9☐

EXPERIENCING TEL AVIV

CHAPTER 14   **99**

ON TO JERUSALEM

CHAPTER 15   **1**☐☐

AL'S ISRAELI NEIGHBORHOOD

CHAPTER 16   **1**☐**8**

CHANUKAH AND CHRISTMAS

CHAPTER 17   **11**☐

AL'S MESSIANIC JUDAISM

CHAPTER 18   **118**

WALKING OLD JERUSALEM

CHAPTER 19   **1**☐**8**

TWO EMPTY TOMBS

CHAPTER 20   **1**☐☐

EVIDENCE AND VERDICT

CHAPTER 21   **1**☐☐

DOWN TO THE SEA IN A VAN

CHAPTER 22   **1**☐**9**

AL'S ALAMO

CHAPTER 23   **15**☐

RETURN TO TEL AVIV

CHAPTER 24   **158**

A MAJOR CRISIS

CHAPTER 25   **1**☐☐

CRISIS MANAGEMENT

CHAPTER 26   **18**☐

CRISIS RESOLUTION

Afterword   **185**

APPENDIX A: ELAINES NOTEBOOK   **19**☐

APPENDIX B: AL'S RESURRECTION EVIDENCE   ☐☐**8**

APPENDIX C: LIZ'S NOTES FOR THE TEMPLE   ☐**1**☐

APPENDIX D: AL'S MESSIANIC CHURCH   ☐**15**

ACKNOWLEGEMENTS   ☐**1**☐

Foreword

The author and I have been in a business alliance for over five years and he is also one of my dearest friends. Hence, I am thrilled and honored to endorse his first book by writing the foreword to it.

Although a work of fiction, at least in its characters and dialogue, this brief but unique crossover book, *1948* posits how the countdown to Armageddon began in the year, 1948. The author, an accomplished educator with degrees in history and theology, reminds us that there is much evidence to sort through regarding our times and where our world is heading. He has done a lot of that sorting out for us and then proceeds to make a solid, interesting case from the evidence. One that compels all of us who value truth, believer or unbeliever alike, to give due consideration to the veracity of the claims of *1948*. Indeed, the book has been designed to assist any person who is serious in giving this evidence, "due consideration." *1948* accomplishes this through the interaction of its Christian and secular characters. Hence, in the process, the work explores thinking on both sides of the argument, from the faith perspective and the secular perspective. The secular view is generally represented by people like George Orwell in his classic work, 1984 and Eric Fromm, who, although brought up in a generally scholarly and accomplished orthodox Jewish family, reputed all of his early instruction in favor of a secular-humanistic philosophy of life.

However, what I enjoy most is that this exploration of opposing ideas is done in an often light hearted and entertaining way. It is a story that is primarily focused on the dialogue of four old friends from their Boston high school days, the Steins and the Morettis and their mutual friend, Al Hoffman, original owner of the 1948 Store. As a follower of these four friends and Al, the reader is led on an interesting journey of ideas, perspectives, historical evidences and predictions, brought out in a way that is relatively easy for all to comprehend.

No one need fear that they must have a PHD in philosophy or Theology to understand *1948*. It is an enjoyable and unique read that I am honored and very happy to commend to one and all.

Bob Holmes, Nationally Acclaimed Motivational Speaker and The World's Leading One-Man Volleyball Team.

CHAPTER 1

WHAT'S IN A NAME?

I have operated The 1948 Store, a fine men's clothing store, located at 266 Boylston Street in downtown Boston, Massachusetts, since the spring of 2005. It was at that time that I purchased it from Albert Stephen "Al" Hoffman, founder and long-time owner of The 1948 Store. So, why is the name 1948? Well, I could tell you that's the year my mother's brother and my Uncle, Carlo Ennio "Carl" Albanese, was born, which is in point of fact true, but that is not the reason. Mom also had three sisters, Clara, Dora and Josie, or the three Zias (aunts) as she would refer to them. Growing up, I remember thinking how poor Uncle Carl didn't have a chance as the baby brother in that family. He was going to be spoiled no matter what.

Or, because it was the year the Miss Boston Diner was started, which is also true. The Miss Boston was a family-owned restaurant in the same neighborhood where my dad, Angelo, and Uncle Carl grew up. It was their favorite local place to hang out. They often told us kids how back in the day everyone went to the

1

movies at the Strand. Then Uncle Carl would always point out, "And then we took our dates back to the Miss Boston. Or, on the weekends we sometimes went to Rhodes on The Charles ballroom and then finished the night at Miss Boston." He always recounted these memories with a smile on his face.

It was open all night, and family-friendly, which was rare in the fifties, even in this town, and it was the model for the hang-out on the show "Happier Days," as Dad would say as a reminder to us. Dad said that there were times he was at the Miss Boston every day, having his sunny-side up eggs, toast and corned beef hash.

Dad loved that place and if I had opened a diner instead of buying a clothing store, that could very well be a great reason to call it the 1948, but that was not in fact the true reason for the name, either. Unfortunately, the Miss Boston was gutted by fire a couple of years back, and only about a month after my dad, Angelo, passed on. I am
simply glad he never had to witness such a sad event.

As a sports fan, I might point out that the store was named 1948 because that was the year Citation won the Triple Crown, Bob Mathias was the big winner at the summer Olympics, Satchel Paige finally pitched in the major leagues, Joe Louis beat Jersey Joe Walcott for the heavyweight boxing title, and the great Babe Ruth died. But then again, that would not be true, either. Although, there were some great pictures of Boston sports' celebrities, with autographs, that lined a whole wall of Al's store. And yes, they were all customers at one time or another. And yes again, Al wanted these pictures to continue to adorn the store after he moved to Israel.

Here is a representative sample of the list of pictures, with autographs to Al hanging on 1948's Store's Wall of Fame. If you are from Boston or love their great sports teams, you'll recognize many of them. If not, you should still recognize most. In any event, here goes…

Ted	Rico	Bob	Tom	Bill
Bobby	Red	David	Dewey	Phil
Dustin	John	Russ	Jim L	Jim R
Carl	Johnny P	Manny	Frank	Dom
Tommy	Johnny M	Carlton	Larry	Kevin

We added one more picture after Al moved to Israel. Yes, Al has the biggest, most prominent picture on the Wall of Fame.

Well, getting back to the store's name selection. Perhaps, it could be best explained in the context of some things that happened

several years ago at The 1948 Store.

CHAPTER 2

A CHANGING OF THE GUARD

I will never forget May 15, 2005. It was the day Al and I finally signed papers at the closing, making The 1948 Store officially mine. Al picked that date, May 15, because it was the 67th birthday of Israel's becoming a modern nation. In any event, the deal was done and my wife Elaine and I were thrilled. Following the closing, Elaine and I went straight to the Top of The Hub Restaurant to celebrate. It is just down from the store and it is also located on Boylston St. As expected, our dinner was superb. The steaks were large, delicious, and just the way we had ordered them. These are true beef cuts with exceptional flavor. Elaine really enjoyed her large baked potato with chives, bacon and sour cream. Our waiter, Vicky, was excellent, too. She was very attentive to all of our needs. The cheesecake desserts-always amazing- were to die for. The Top of The Hub has always been one of our favorite go-to spots for a romantic or celebratory dinner. The food is consistently fabulous, as is the ambiance. I had called ahead for a reservation and a booth and they had one ready and waiting upon our arrival. Vicky even took a picture of the two of us, and later gave it to us in a heart-shaped frame because we told Vicky that we were celebrating a special occasion. Then, in a larger envelope, she presented copies of it and a few other pictures she had taken, along with a handwritten congratulatory note. All this was totally unprompted or requested. It is this "extra mile" type of stuff that makes the Top of The Hub so special. So, once again, they made a special night memorable for Elaine and me.

Besides enjoying this fabulous meal, Elaine was really anxious to discuss details of taking over the business from Al, so that was the center of our discussion for the entire evening.

Elaine, ever the cautious one, wanted to know how I planned to proceed in the transition phase. I assured her that Al had already agreed to work for a minimum of six months at the store before he moved to Israel. And he would be introducing me personally to regular customers, and walk me through all the various aspects that I needed to learn about operations at the store. I was also able to share with her that Hugo Fratelli, Al's long-time valued tailor, was also going to stay on with us. Hugo was reserved and spoke broken English, having moved to Boston from Florence, Italy, some thirty years earlier. He was also a superb tailor, very well-versed in the fashions of fine men's clothing. I would come to appreciate Hugo as a trusted confidante and advisor in the years ahead. We ended that dinner at the outstanding Top of The Hub, with a toast…

"Buona fortuna a cent anni, se Dio Voule, per Il Nogozzio 1948!" I said in my best broken Italian.

"Whatever does that mean?" asked Elaine.

"Oh, what I was trying to say is, 'May there be good fortune for The 1948 Store for 100 years, God willing; at least those were my sentiments,' " I explained.

"It sure sounded good to me." Elaine responded kindly.

"In the old country, they would call me the Nogozziniere, or shop keeper," I said proudly.

"Maybe to your face," Elaine joked.

Our night out did not quite end over dinner; an even more romantic conclusion to the evening followed upon our return home. Once we got to the front door of our house, I spontaneously picked Elaine up and carried her over the threshold, just like the day we were married. Once inside, I took her straight to the living room and gently placed her on the couch. I had a large cake, some chocolate covered strawberries, and a dozen roses waiting for us, too. Then, I lit some candles and turned on some soft romantic music. All our favorite legends including Frank, Dean, and Tony, sang just for us, as we danced the rest of the night away. We also had some crazy fun feeding cake slices and chocolate strawberries to each other.

CHAPTER 3

PROFESSOR AL

By now you are probably wondering when I am going to get to the real reason for naming the store 1948. Soon and very soon, as the old song goes. It has so much to do with the previous owner, Albert Stephen Hoffman, that before I reveal the real reason for the name, I must reveal the real Al Hoffman to you, for it to make any sense.

I had been in discussions with Al Hoffman about purchasing his store for a very long time, before actually buying the place. I had worked in retail around Boston for my entire career and now I wanted the chance to run my own shop. I guess it was just part of my American dream. I had known Al for years, both as a customer and as a fellow member of Lexington Community Church. That's the unusual part, or actually just one of several unique aspects of this story. Sometime in the early '90s, Al had become a dedicated believer in Jesus Christ as Lord and Savior, or in other words — a Messianic Jew. It had led us into some deep religious discussions over the years. Besides that facet of our relationship, Al always

9

stocked quality clothing at very reasonable prices. He also always gave a "family and friends" discount, which was a nice enticement. The fact is, I always thought being counted as one of Al's friends was an honor. He is one of those people who is very hard not to like. Every time I entered the small but friendly confines of Al's store, Al was always there to greet me with a, "Hey bud, how's it going? How about a quick cup of coffee? Juice, pop, what's your pleasure? Maria just baked some fantastic cookies!" Maria was Al's wife and she was now deceased. Al was not a very tall man, more on the short and stocky side. He did not have a handsome face either. As Al once said to me, "My face does not lend itself to Hollywood posters and magazine covers, so I prefer my likeness to be rarely taken." However, that was not the sum of this beautiful person. The true portrait of this man was magnificent to all of us who knew, loved and respected him. Al was a man without guile, as Jesus might say. His character was beyond reproach. He did not cheat, steal, lie; stuck to his wife faithfully and loved his only child Sonia, devotedly. Sadly, Sonia died in an automobile accident a few years back.

Al was also a self-taught theologian, very informed in regard to doctrine, history, archeology, science and all other subjects

10

pertinent to understanding Scripture. That knowledge, along with his natural ability as a teacher and his warm friendly personality, made him quite interesting and engaging when discussing things he was passionate about. And God, Scripture and end-time theories and ideas were all subjects that Al was most passionate about.

I vividly recall his generally impromptu lesson one day when I was in his back office. It was on an interesting topic, but one that I was totally unfamiliar with: blood moons. Here is what Al had to say,

"I base this teaching on some prophetic writing from the book of Luke, where it states: 'There shall be signs in the sun, moon, and stars and on the earth distress of nations...men's hearts failing them for fear and expectation of the things that are coming on the earth, for the powers of heaven shall be shaken. And then shall they see the Son of Man coming in a cloud with power and great glory. And when these things begin to come to pass, look up and lift up your heads, for your redemption draweth nigh.' "

Luke 21:25-28

Going on from that reading, he launched right into his lesson for the day on blood moons. I will at least try to paraphrase the lesson here. It was a great example of this man's great capacity for teaching, especially on things biblical.

Along with many other biblical scholars-- and make no mistake about it — Al Hoffman was an outstanding biblical scholar, albeit a self-taught one, Al maintained that these signs and wonders will help Christians know that Christ soon will be returning to earth. Al was always quick to point out that even though we understand that no one can know the exact day and time, Christ did teach that we can know generally when he will be returning, by the signs of the times. Al really thought blood moons had a lot to do with what Jesus was talking about regarding signs and wonders.

Here are the salient points of what I recall about our talk that day.

"The first thing people need to understand, Joe, is that the sun, moon, and stars are used throughout the entire Bible as indicators or signs that an event or a season is near," Al began.

"Do you mean like astrological signs that so many people look to today for guidance?" I asked.

"Well, yes and no. Yes, astrology has signs and one can make some general correlations to months and personality types, especially if you get very creative. However, I believe these are really a counterfeit, like much else of what is humanly or demonically inspired as alternative belief systems to Judeo-Christian historical truth," Al responded.

"So, you're saying the signs and wonders pointed out in the Scriptures, both Old and New Testaments, are the real deal," I stated.

"Exactly, Joe. Just recall from your time in Sunday school, how it was a star that led the wise men to the newborn Jesus. Or, how about when the sun 'stood still' when the mighty Joshua led Israel to victory in war? I truly believe that we are going to see God using more of these types of signs again, as the end times lead to the return of Christ to earth," asserted Al, the teacher.

"It seems as if many people are getting a sense that things are changing, whether it's climate change, more frequent and more devastating earthquakes, hurricanes, droughts, as well as geopolitical changes, such as the fall of the Soviet bloc and the new aggressiveness of Russia and Iran, two major enemies of Israel; and on it goes," I responded.

"You're right. Things are a-changing, as they say, and I believe that God is using such upheavals to communicate with us in

13

supernatural ways again, as He did so long ago," said Al.

As Al went on to explain it, blood moons are not an uncommon or strange phenomenon. In fact, they have been recognized occurrences for a long time. However, from the Judeo-Christian perspective, it seems that every time there has been a blood moon something significant has happened to the people of Israel. In our era, many students of the topic have been predicting the next blood moons will be taking place during the years 2014 and 2015, so it is becoming a timely subject again, at least for believers. In fact, the national media reported that one of these happened on April 14, 2014. Scholars who have studied this, including Al, point out that the appearance of four so close together is unusual. Although very rare, when they do occur they come in the spring and the fall of a single year. The first recorded blood moon was about 500 years ago, and there were several back in the 1940s, just before Israel became a nation.

"So," I asked Al, "what exactly does a blood moon look like?"

"To put it quite simply, a blood moon is when a reddish shadow is cast upon the moon by the Earth," Explained Al.

14

"How does that exactly happen?" I asked.

"Well, I'm no scientist, so I can't give you a textbook explanation but the way I understand it is when our earth is in a certain position between the sun and the moon, as the sun shines through the earth's atmosphere it reflects back to us what appears to be the moon looking a deep red color. Hence the name, blood moon," Explained Al.

"Well, okay, but what exactly has that to do with anything regarding end times, and us humans?" I asked.

Al launched into a very lengthy explanation, and I was all ears.

"So called blood moons occurred periodically throughout Scripture. We see one in the book of Joel, where he describes "...the sun being turned to darkness and the moon to blood before the coming of the great and dreadful day of the Lord."

In the New Testament book of Acts, Peter refers to the verse in Joel and connects it with the tribulation and end times. In the book of Revelation, the writer John also connects blood moons to a tribulation period that may take place prior to Christ's return to earth."

"Wow, I never made that connection in my mind before," I exclaimed.

"As it happened, blood moons appeared last in April 2014, around Easter and Passover and they came back again in September 2014, which coincides with the Jewish Feast of Tabernacles. They came back again at approximately the same dates in 2015. Those back-to- back occurrences are extremely rare," Al said.

"Interestingly enough, several years ago I was watching the evening news as usual when Brian Williams of NBC News mentioned that blood moons would be seen during the days around Easter. I was amazed, as I listened to him on Monday evening, April 14, 2014. So, they are for real," I remarked.

"In times past, blood moons always were followed closely by events that either directly or indirectly affected the people of Israel. Al cited the fact that blood moons were recorded around the time of Columbus' discovering the New World. While it was a perilous time for the Jews as they were being thrown out of Spain during the late 1400s, the New World eventually became a haven for them. In the twentieth century, America helped the Jews by leading the allies to victory in WWII, and was also instrumental in helping the Jewish people to establish Israel in 1948," Al stated.

There is no doubt in Al's mind that this was a key reason why God so blessed America since its birth as a nation. As Al shared with me his passion for this topic, it became clear to me why his store was named The 1948 Store. It was simply the most significant year in the life of one Albert Stephen Hoffman – lover of his Jewish heritage, lover of Israel as a modern nation, and lover of Yeshua as his Messiah.

CHAPTER 4

MENTOR AL

The Saturday after the closing I was at work bright and early, at 9 am. Although the store did not open until 10 am, Al and Hugo had both arrived around 8 am. They started to dust, vacuum, put out new stock, rearrange old stock, start the coffee, and take care of the 101 details it seemed to take to get the doors open at 10 am. This was my first major lesson as the new owner of this wonderful little store; as fun and enjoyable as this dream come true was, it also was going to be a lot of hard work and a lot of paying attention to details.

We were busy all morning and soon it was time for lunch. Al asked Hugo to watch the front and motioned for me to follow him back to what was now my office.

"You rely on Hugo for quite a bit more than just tailoring suits, don't you, Al?" I asked.

"Absolutely, and you will have to as well. Hugo is reserved, but he knows clothes and he knows the clothing business and he knows this store like no one else in this world, besides me," Al answered candidly.

18

"Tell me a bit about him," I said.

"Hugo is very dependable and a man of great integrity and honesty. He has old-world pride and sensibilities. To Hugo, right is right and wrong is wrong. He is also disciplined, always dressed in perfectly matched tailored suit, tie, and shined shoes. I think his cologne, also named Hugo, is appropriately applied and freshened each day that he is on the floor. He truly adds a professional dimension to the business that says quality, if you know what I mean. I never could have built this store successfully without one Hugo Fratelli, Italian Catholic from the old country," Al said, speaking emotionally.

"Wow, that's quite an endorsement," I responded.

"And one more thing, my Italian heritage friend; do you know what Fratelli means in Italiano?" Al asked me.

"Oh, I am pretty sure it means brothers," I responded.

"You're spot on, and that is exactly how you will learn to trust Hugo Fratelli, like a brother," Al offered.

Then Al transitioned right back into a store orientation. As he pointed out, The 1948 Store was built on a reputation of quality and personalized service. It stocked a lot of great names and it was going to be hard to eliminate any of them. We're talking a sizable list and these were just the jackets and suits: Armani, Hickey Freeman, Isaia Napoli, Joseph Abboud, Polo, and Zanclla, to name only a few.

Then Al took me through his inventory of the various brands that we stocked in other categories. Our store categories, besides our suits and jackets, included the following: accessories, jeans, neckwear, shirts and pants.

The reality was beginning to set in, that I had purchased and now was fully responsible for a 3,000-square-foot men's store on Bolyston Street in the heart of Boston. It helped that the store was within walking distance of many financial businesses and not too far from high-rise office buildings and the courts. After all, we knew the bankers, corporate leaders, and lawyers had to dress for success in their daily work and that was a key to our success.

Al further explained that most high-end suits are from Italy and about ninety-five percent of the store's suits, shirts, and ties are made there. Though Jewish, Al also shared my love affair with all things Italian, and he taught me that much in the clothing business had to do with that Italian clothing mystique and our customers' passion for the Italian lines.

Hugo even makes some of his own suits. I never knew that prior to buying the store. I guess as a middle-income customer, I was only shown the lower to middle end of the inventory. So, I never knew that our most expensive suit is a fine wool, priced at $5,000.

To me, the store was beautiful, but to Elaine it was in need of a woman's touch. She pointed out certain details that would make it more appealing to the women, who so often accompanied the men. To her eyes, the store was a clean space, but a bit cluttered; ties were on rods and hung on walls throughout the store but there is no tie section, as she pointed out to me. Dress shirts were stacked to near-ceiling on all the side walls. However, there was a method to Al's madness, as I pointed out to her. Al believed that with few signs and little rhyme or reason to the merchandise layout, two things would occur: first, customers would focus on the beautiful merchandise and not the ambiance, and secondly, they would be inclined to ask for help from our sales people. It's strictly a store for men who want a no-nonsense environment. As I would often say to Elaine, it is after all a *men's* store and our male customers did not seem to mind. Still, Elaine would come down after her days at school and help me with decorating and better organizing of the store. It was something Al and I just graciously put up with. And besides, it was not his store to worry about anymore and I was not about to upset our happy home. And, we knew she just wanted to be a part of things at the store; but after she left, we would just allow things to get back to our comfort level, at least to some degree.

In any event, this Saturday routine with Al became an almost daily one for the next six months, as Al made sure that I understood and knew everything about the store and the fine men's clothing business that he had learned through so many decades. I thought that I knew clothing, but owning a store and knowing how to order and market took things to a whole new level, and I could not have asked for a better mentor than Al Hoffman.

CHAPTER 5

OLD FRIENDS REUNITE

As I recall, it was a typical windy and brisk Boston autumn day in the late fall. Al had moved to Israel a few years back. So, it was just Hugo and me holding down the fort, along with one part-time sales person. The part-time sales person was my only son, Dan, a 31 year old father of two and a sociologist by training. Dan was a fine young family man, but had hardened his heart towards the claims of Christ. That fact was a constant source of concern and heartache to his mother and me. But, I digress: we were taking inventory of all the items in an effort to try to see what was selling and what was not. In any event, it was sometime early in the afternoon of that day, when a customer walked into the store looking to buy some suits, ties, shirts, and accessories., as I overhead him say to Hugo. Now, the man looked somewhat familiar to me from across the store and when I approached him the customer's large dark brown eyes widened as he fixed his gaze on me. I was sure that this customer was none other than my old high school buddy, Billy Stein.

"Bill," I said incredulously, "Bill Stein, is that you?"

"Joe Moretti," he exclaimed!

I grinned, "How many years has it been?"

"Wow, we lost touch after high school and I never knew you worked at 1948," Bill said.

"Work here, Billy; I own the joint. Well, at least since the spring of 2005, when I took over from the owner, Al Hoffman. Before that I sold clothing at other retailers around Boston," I responded.

"Oh, I knew Al quite well, since I used to shop here regularly when I was first building my medical practice up in Lexington," offered Bill.

After a brief pause he added, "It's my first time back in a long while though."

I then introduced Bill to Dan and Hugo. Hugo remembered Bill as a customer that he hadn't seen for some time.

And Dan quipped, "So, you're the guy that I heard so many stories about while growing up."

"Well, now I can tell you which ones were true," Bill kidded.

Bill and I were left alone and we began to recall the good old days of the mid-1970s at Boston's Lane Polytech High School, home of the mighty Falcons!

"Remember all the fun we had in Mr. A's history class and playing baseball together?" I asked.

"Yeah, he never could tell where the spit balls were coming from or that we were throwing them," Bill commented.

"Hey, you know Joe, I sure thought you would end up in the majors with that golden right pitching arm that you had back then," Bill went on.

"Well, a torn rotator cuff during my freshmen year at Northeastern kind of ended that dream," I replied.

"Hey, remember us double-dating to the Senior Prom in your dad's new Lincoln Town Car? You with Liz Levinski and me with Elaine?" I asked.

"Do I ever remember? I had to promise my dad that I would work at his pharmacy all summer, as both the janitor and the stock boy, just to let me drive the thing. I never told you, but he actually wanted to drive us to the prom and pick us up," Bill told me.

"I'm sure glad you didn't let that happen! It was a great night and Elaine and I went on to date while I was at Northeastern, then we got married four years later. Now it's one grown kid and two grand kids all these years later," I said proudly.

"I got married to Liz during medical school at Yale, but we never had any kids. We thought long and hard about adopting, but ultimately decided against it. I guess we were just too head long into our respective careers. But it's all good, as they say. We have had a full and enjoyable life." Billy explained, with a wonderful laugh, also reminiscent of the "good old days."

"A doctor!" I said enthusiastically. "Wow, what kind? No, let me guess, a psychiatrist?" I kidded.

"No, but I did study psycho-ceramics at Brown University, in Providence, where I did my undergrad work," Billy said jokingly.

"Psycho-ceramics, what kind of course is that?" I asked, playing right along like Bill's straight man.

Bill, with a coy expression, responded that it was the study of "cracked pots."

"Silly as ever, Bill; or excuse me, Doctor Stein," I commented.

"Oh come on Joe. It will always be just Bill between us," Bill said.

26

"By the way, Bill, what kind of medicine do you practice?" I inquired.

"Well, if you must know, I am a Dr. of Urology," Bill responded.

"Oh, I know about you guys and your PSA tests and prostate exams. Not fun stuff for us males of the species. What is it, about one out of three that needs to see guys like you?" I questioned.

"Something like that. I hope you are doing okay in that area. You are, aren't you?" Bill queried, acting like the caring doctor he no doubt is.

"Yes sir! Just fine so far," I responded, not admitting the whole truth that I underwent an operation a couple of years back, for prostate cancer. That was just getting too personal for me.

"Good. But if you ever want a second professional opinion, just let me know," Bill offered, in a way that led me to believe that he wasn't buying my response completely.

Then after an awkward pause, Bill continued...

"I don't have a lot of time right now, so let me get the suits and shirts I came in here for and then I will be back after they're altered and we can make plans to get together," Bill suggested.

"Absolutely," I said. "And at some point we'll have to make plans to get together with Elaine and Liz, too," I said.

"That would be great!" Bill positively responded.

And with that conversation, we began to rekindle our old friendship.

Bill bought a few items, including the suits, which he would have to come back for after Hugo tailored them. I gave him a twenty percent "family and friend" discount. We then agreed to catch up more when he came back downtown for his tailored suits.

CHAPTER 6

CATCHING UP

About a month later, during our busy Christmas season, I was working in the back office when Hugo came in and said Bill was here for his suits and was wondering if I had a moment.

"Sure, send him back here," I responded.

A few moments later, in walked Bill.

"Hey Doctor, are you happy with your new suits?" I asked.

"Delighted!" he exclaimed.

"It's almost lunch time," I observed, looking at my watch.

"There are so many great restaurants in this area. So, I'll let you choose one," said Bill.

"And if you can break away now, Bill's buying at Davido's," said Bill.

"Can't pass that up. Hugo can watch the store. Let's go," I responded.

We walked down several blocks from our Boylston Street store front to Davido's Italian Restaurant in the North End of the city, along the way having a light and positive conversation about the good old days of high school at Lane Polytech.

"Oh, you really do like nostalgia, Joe!" Bill kidded.

Once we had arrived and were seated in Davido's, Bill reminisced about all the times we had come to this place on dates and occasionally for pizza after I had pitched in a big game for Lane Polytech.

It didn't take us long to make our choice and order a couple of chicken parmigiano lunches. Then we continued catching up on the last three decades. After a fun trip down the nostalgia road, Bill and I began to share on a little deeper level. It began with Al Hoffman, 1948's previous owner, who had sold me the business and moved to Israel.

"So, Joe, you never did catch me up on Al Hoffman. Is he alive and well?" Bill asked.

"As far as I know, he's doing fine, but you'll never guess where he's living now," I responded.

"Oh, I bet I could. Remember, I told you that I used to come in to The 1948 Store quite a bit, and my old Jewish friend shared his dream with me on more than one occasion. So, did Al do it? Did he really move to Israel?" guessed Bill.

"You nailed it, Billy. Al Hoffman is now living in his beloved Israel,"

I responded again.

"Like I said, I knew moving to Israel someday was his great dream, and of course, that is why he named his store 1948. That was the year Israel became a nation," Bill commented.

"I've got to tell you, Joe, I share that dream with Al. I guess a lot of us Jews do. I don't know exactly why, but I guess it's just an inexplicable emotional tug to be in the land of our people, now that it has been restored to us," Bill went on.

"I guess I can understand that to some degree. Even many Christians long to visit the Holy Land, and many thousands do each year; and yes, some have moved there for religious reasons," I said.

"Funny, Joe, it is only one small place, but it means so much, to so many, for entirely different reasons," Bill observed astutely.

"Yes, and let's not forget the Muslims, who see the same land as a place of religious importance as well, especially Jerusalem," I mentioned.

"Yes Joe, but the Holy Land you and the Muslims refer to belongs to Israel today, and they also see Mecca and Medina as holy

31

places, too. Jews recognize only one, Jerusalem. I am a secular Jew, but even I know that much," said Bill.

"No, you're absolutely right. It all began thousands of years ago, when Jews and Christians assert that the God of Abraham first gave him the Promised Land in and around Jerusalem. They have been attacked on all sides and by all major empires, going back to the first ones. It's been going on for centuries, right into the modern era," I soberly commented.

"My people have had problems with the Egyptians ever since," said Bill.

"And, Bill, from the Jewish perspective — and the vast majority of Christians support that point of view as well-the persecution of your people started even before the Egyptian empire. It started with the Assyrian empire; the very first empire in recorded history. And of course, the murder of six million Jews, orchestrated by the Nazis during World War II, was the last great effort to destroy the Jewish people. Biblical warnings from both your Old Testament and our New Testament, inform us that it won't be the last, either" I commented.

"Oh, I don't know about biblical warnings. It just seems to

be our Jewish "Manifest Destiny." Especially, when the third great religion born in the Middle East, Islam, has extremists elements in it that want to destroy us. And, as you know, tensions run high, when religious convictions run so deep," said Bill.

"That's all part of what Elaine and I want to explore with you. No one can deny that it is an interesting and timely topic," I said.

"No, you're right, Joe, but we didn't come to Davido's to have a deep religious and geo-political discussion, just some chicken and pasta." Bill paused for a moment. "However, having said that, I do have to share one more thing along those lines with you."

"I was wondering why you weren't eating more of your lunch. The old Bill would have it devoured by now," I teased Bill.

"Bill answered softly and thoughtfully. Those suits and clothing items that I bought the other day, they're not needed here. I am closing my practice in the U.S. and Liz and I are moving to Israel."

Surprised, I asked, "Are you absolutely sure that is what you want to do?

I am sure that you have thought about it long and hard."

"Oh yes, more than anything else in the world, Liz and I want to follow that tug on our hearts back to Israel and to be with our people living there." Bill responded.

"When are you moving?" I asked.

"Our goal is to be there next year, so we are still many months away. However, we are closing down the practice by March 1, and Liz is quitting her job by April 1st. We need to sell the house and some other properties and also settle a number of things before we depart for Israel," Bill said.

"That's only months away. Wow, that is not what I expected to hear. What type of work does Liz do?" I asked.

"She is a highly regarded Solid Design Architect for Andrews & Passeroni Associates," replied Bill.

"Andrews & Passeroni Associates-they have built some of the biggest and best buildings in Boston," I recalled.

"That's right, and Liz has worked as the chief oversight manager on a number of their major design/ build projects such as skyscrapers, schools and smaller office buildings both in Boston and around the country; in cities like New York, L.A., and Chicago," Bill continued. Her boss, CEO Gary Passeroni, gave her a wonderful

34

recommendation letter for the Israelis. He pointed to some of Liz's great professional qualities. For example, he wrote that she was exceptional on detail planning, timely on project delivery, held closely to budget projections, was efficient on project coordination and prompt and fair in client services," Bill pointed out proudly.

"You can't be recommended or respected more highly than that in any field,"

I commented.

"Look, it's going to take me more time to digest this than the chicken parm and I do have to get back to the store to relieve Hugo soon. But this discussion is something that we need to continue," I insisted.

"Sure, if you feel that way Joe," Bill said.

"I sure do and it is a very timely topic, given what you just told me. Besides, you and Liz are not the only ones who have been looking closely at Israel. Elaine and I have done a lot of reading and talking on the topic over the years, too. We would love to share some of these things with you and also learn from your perspective," I said.

"I don't know Joe. Are you going to try to convert us to some sort of fundamentalist Christianity? Because we're not up for that at all." Bill warned.

"I promise you Billy, we love you too much to try to proselytize you guys to another religious point of view. Elaine and I see ourselves as Christian believers — people who are imperfect, but who have our sins paid for and forgiven because of what Christ, our Savior, did on the cross. And, we are serious and not people of nominal Christian faith," I explained.

"So, if you ever want to know more about our personal beliefs, just ask. Other than that we won't go there, except as our faith relates to Israel. Is that okay?" I offered.

"Okay, but just so you know, Liz and I are not active in our Judaism and never attend Synagogue. I guess you would call us more ethnic or cultural Jews," Bill responded.

"Enough with the labels already! Will you come over to our house for dinner after the holidays? Elaine makes a great sauce. She learned it from my mother, Viola, when we were first married," I said.

"Viola Moretti," Billy affirmed, "now she was a great Italian cook! How is she doing?"

"Oh yes, you spent a lot of time at our dinner table and my mom loved every minute of it. Sadly, Bill, she is no longer with us. She passed on several years back...but her cooking lives on, mostly through Elaine," I commented.

"You persuaded me with that offer. Liz and I will be there; just name the day and time," Bill promised.

"Billy Stein, are you telling me, Momma Viola's meals of times past, made this an offer you could not refuse?" I joked.

"Oh, let's stop with the Guido routine right there, Joe. I remember how you made me sit through the first Godfather movie, like a dozen times, and then always tried to imitate Marlon Brando by putting cotton in your mouth. But let's just agree that Momma Viola's sauce is too great to miss out on, even if I have to put up with your antics again to enjoy it," Bill kidded.

And with that, we both laughed. Bill picked up the check as he had said he would, and he even paid the tip. We set the tentative time for our dinner with the wives while we walked back to the store. Then we headed our separate ways.

"I'll call you after the holidays and after I confirm the date with my boss at home, and I suggest you do the same with yours," I joked as we parted company.

CHAPTER 7

DINNER AT THE MORETTIS

Dinner finally happened at our house in early February, after much back and forth, trying to coordinate our busy schedules. Bill and Liz arrived right on time with a present for us. Actually, it was a present of new vinyl records for us of a number of our favorite singers, such as Frank, Dean, Louie, and Tony. Along with it, they gave us a brand new turntable to play it on. We were blown away, as they say.

"They say vinyl is coming back," said Liz.

"Yeah and we were hoping we could get to dance a little tonight. Just like at the prom," said Bill.

"You guys are too much," said Elaine.

I remember thinking, what a wonderful, thoughtful couple.

Once dinner finally did get under way, it was just like back at prom night. We picked up where we had left off decades ago. And after the evening was over and our guests had left, Elaine said she thought Bill had changed quite a bit, but not so much, Liz. I agreed. Both of us thought that Liz remained the same as in high school: an attractive, petite women, with a pleasant smile and charming personality to boot. She also revealed herself to be bright, witty, well read and a person of firm convictions. And above all, it was clear that she still made my friend Bill very happy.

We enjoyably rekindled our relationship that night and finished with some old fashion dancing like on prom night so many years ago.

This was part of the conversation of the evening, as I recall it.

"Remember the little secret we found out at the prom?" Liz queried.

Bill looked puzzled, "Whatever are you talking about?"

"Oh, I bet I know," Elaine said, with a smile that roused our curiosity. And then she went on to explain...

"Joe and I had just started dating and I was able to hide it from him at first, but once we spent such a long time at the prom and the teachers allowed it and..."

"Just spit it out," I interrupted, playfully.

"I finally just took out my pack of Pall-Mall cigarettes and lit one up. You, never saw such an astonished look on Joe's face. I liked Joe, and thought; this is it, he either is going to learn to live with it, or this is our last time together, but I am just going to die if I can't smoke with all the other smokers at our table, who were blowing it in my face," said Elaine.

"Oh, I remember that," Bill contributed. "Joe never stopped talking about it for weeks. And you were right, he wasn't sure he could continue to date you. I remember thinking how glad I was that school was ending or I might never stop hearing about it."

"You're right Bill, but obviously I got over it and I am glad I did, because it certainly turned out to be the right decision," I responded warmly, as I glanced at Elaine.

"By the way, do you guys care if I light up here at the table?" Elaine asked.

"Now, honey? It really is just like the prom. D'eja' vu all over again," I said.

"As a medical doctor, I really have to tell you of my concerns over inhaling secondary smoke. You see," Bill said, trying to sound his professional best...

"There you go, Billy, tweaked again and this time by the other Moretti. Elaine stopped smoking years ago. Come on now Bill,

41

do you think we would've gone on dating if she hadn't? Not in those days, with my strict Christian parents," I commented.

Everyone was now enjoying a good laugh.

"One thing is for sure, for being Scotch, you definitely learned to cook a great Italian meal. I remember this sauce taste from when I hung out at Momma Viola's kitchen whenever I could," Bill commented.

"Yes, what a great meal you put on for us tonight... game hens, bracciola, stuffed peppers, gnocchi, eggplant parmegiano, pasta fagioli soup and all the rest," exclaimed Liz.

"Oh, thanks but you're so right, I learned from the best. And thanks for saying I'm Scotch, Bill, but actually I am Scottish, scotch is the drink." said Elaine.

"I've just been tweaked again, haven't I?" Bill humbly asked.

"Yup, that's twice tonight," I said, with laughs all around.

"You know I'm keeping score and I WILL get you back, so be for warned," Bill responded.

"Yeah, yeah," said Liz, "and then she went on to question Elaine.

"What I want to know is just what you do when you're not

Chef Moretti?"

"Oh, nothing too exciting, at least most of the time. I teach American and English literature at good old Lane Polytech," responded Elaine.

"That's not an easy job, but you must find it rewarding," commented Bill.

"Oh yeah, I do, but..." began Elaine.

"She just doesn't enjoy it when she gets kids like Billy and I were back in the day," I finished her thought.

"I wasn't exactly going to say that, but now that you mention it..." Elaine responded.

"Oh, we didn't turn out so bad," I blurted out, as I started chasing Billy into the living room with a kitchen towel that I just grabbed.

Another good laugh was had by all.

"Boys, boys, calm down and sit down-NOW!" Elaine said loudly, in the command-presence voice of a strict teacher. "And when you do, I'll be in with the desert, homemade cannoli and ice cream, or should we say gelato?" Elaine said with a stern look.

"Yes, Mrs. Moretti," Bill and I said in unison, sheepishly.

We all laughed once again and then Bill and I sat down in the living room, while Liz helped Elaine in the kitchen. It just took a few minutes and then in came the ladies with the goodies. After we finished off the dolci and espresso, the talk turned to the Steins' big decision to move to Israel.

"So, now I have a secret to tell," Liz volunteered.

"Uh boy," I said with a smile. "Here it comes...ah, whatever 'it is,' as a former President might say."

"Sorry if I built up your curiosity too much. 'It' is no big scandalous secret. Bill and I agreed that the next time we all were together, we should tell you the most important reason we are moving to Israel. As you now know, I spent my career years as an architectural engineer. In that capacity, I helped engineer some of the major buildings in Boston, Chicago, New York, and L.A. including some of their biggest buildings," Liz said.

"So, what are you telling us, Liz? Are they going to start building giant skyscrapers in Jerusalem? Is that what this is all about?" I asked.

"Not exactly," said Bill, "It is much more important than that kind of project. And it was Al that first started the wheels turning

44

and now that he has lived over there for a while..."

"Will one of you please spit it out, this is getting too dramatic," I interrupted.

"The Israeli government has asked me to work on the re-building of the Temple," Liz blurted out.

"That is incredible!" exclaimed Elaine. "As a Christian, that gives me goose bumps."

"Absolutely thrilling!" I added.

"It is just one more religious structure and there are already so many in the Holy Land. So, although it will be challenging and important, it isn't all that significant in the big scheme of things," Liz stated.

"Not that significant? To Christians, it is thrilling and fantastic because it has been so long predicted as one of the signs of the times for the second coming of Christ to Earth," Elaine responded.

"Really?" said Liz. "You have got to be kidding me."

"Of course, Liz and I, as secular Jews, don't believe in Jesus as a deity and certainly not his return to earth. But, you know we agreed to hear you out, concerning what you see happening Israel, as long as you don't try to convert us; so why don't you just get started?" explained Bill.

"Yes, I am looking forward to hearing your point of view." Liz added.

"Let's start right there, with the rebuilding of the Jewish Temple in Jerusalem." I said.

With that, we began to introduce the broad topic of historic Jewish and Christian teachings on world events; both prior to and following the second coming of Jesus Christ. These events that would ultimately culminate in Israel, during the last days of earth as we know it.

"According to our view, the rebuilding of the Temple has always been pointed to as one of the most significant end time events, as Christians often refer to them. These are the events that would signify that the return of Christ was close at hand." I started to explain.

"Now, how do you come to that conclusion?" asked Bill.

"The clear indication from all of our prophetic warnings is that Solomon's great Temple will be re-built on the same site where it existed in Solomon's day, and when it is, all the old-time religious sacrifices of the Jews will be practiced again by Orthodox Jews, in accordance with the Old Mosaic law," I responded.

"That does not sound too ominous," commented Bill.

"Seemingly so. However, it is at that time that the rest of the Middle East, along with a confederation of European powers, under a new but diabolical leader, will come against Israel. His armies will once again try to destroy Israel and in the process he will put an end to the sacrifices and worship of God, all at the same time. However, this time, instead of destroying the Temple, this diabolical leader will try to use it as a place where he will be worshipped. Because at that point, he is going to reveal himself as the world's only true religious leader, too. This person is the anti-Christ or agent of Satan, with demonic powers from him," I explained.

"You say that the Temple is going to be re-built on the same site as in Solomon's day, but I have been hearing from Al that this might not be possible, since a large Islamic Mosque and the Dome of The Rock Mosque both sit on or nearby the site of the Temple Mount today. There's no way the Muslims are going to stand still for their worship centers to be replaced by a Jewish one," Liz stated emphatically.

"You're absolutely correct, Liz, and that is something that may take a miracle, but there is at least one reason to think that a simple down-to-earth solution might be negotiable. The actual site of Solomon's Temple is now believed by many to be about 150 yards away from the Dome of The Rock. Mosque, which could mean that the whole problem could be avoided without any major cultural upheaval," Elaine said.

"Al never mentioned that fact. I will have to ask him about it," Liz commented.

"Oh, we are sure excited for you two," Elaine went on. "This upcoming trip, and subsequent move, is all just so exciting to Joe and me, and we're not even going. You must be thrilled beyond measure. And who knows, maybe Liz will be the miracle that God will use to locate the Temple in just the right spot. And with you being able to find out first-hand information from Al and sharing it with us...wow!" Elaine blurted out, excitedly.

"Now, come on, miracles with Liz? Let's stay within reality bounds, please. And, of course we'll gladly share as much as we can. But I am sure Liz will have communication restrictions placed upon her," cautioned Bill.

"Of course, and please excuse our excitement," I said. "We understand. So back to the major issue of why the rebuilding of the Temple is so important to Christians. It is because once the Temple is finally rebuilt and ancient sacrifice practices commence, we believe it will trigger the retaliation of a coalition of countries, led by a powerful and ruthless political and religious dictator. Jealous of the sacrificial worship of God, he will move against Israel to destroy the sacrifices of the Temple and replace them with a worship of himself. This is all according to Daniel's Old Testament prophecy," I said.

"Ah, so your saying that not only the rebuilding of the Temple, but a major desecration of it, will signal to Christians that Christ's return is near?" Bill questioned.

"Yes, and exactly three and one-half years later," interjected Elaine.

"And to think, Al, you and Liz are going to be involved in it all. Oh, but then...well, you will all be over there for the rest of what follows. That will be dangerous!"

"Back up, please," said Liz. "What did you mean by exactly three-and-one-half years?"

49

"According to our view," Elaine explained, "when this desecration of the Temple takes place, the return of Christ is only three-and-one-half years away. However, other serious Christians hold to different interpretations of the timing as it relates to Christ's return."

"Yes, but only if all this were true. I'm afraid it would take a lot more than some words written in some religious books, hundreds or even thousands of years ago, to convince me. By the way, you say it was Daniel in the Old Testament, but who was it in your New Testament that predicted all of this happening?" asked Liz.

"In the New Testament it was actually Christ himself that predicted it. And when he did, he warned that those who were in Jerusalem should flee to the mountains, because the destruction and persecution would be intense and widespread," I responded. "And by the way, you're right about-how did you say it-'If it were just some words written in some religious book, hundreds or even thousands of years ago.' It is so much more than that, because the evidence really comes from various sources, not just prophecy. I would like to take a few minutes to explain in detail if I could. Would that be okay?" I asked.

"Sure, all of this makes for interesting conversation, especially in light of our move to Israel, but it's getting late and I am going to start nodding off. I'm afraid that after engaging in that great Italian meal and the dolci that followed, I'm ready for night-night," the good doctor candidly stated.

"Bill's probably right, but I do find this fascinating and I do want to hear more, and this time at our place, maybe in a couple of weeks," Liz said.

With that, we all agreed to continue on with our "conversation," but to shift communications mode a bit. However first, we opened our new records, turned on the player and took the floor to dance, dance, dance, once again.

Before our guests left and since we had the most background and information to share on the topic, it was agreed that I was to map out further issues and questions, by email, over the next week. After that everyone else could ask questions or just opine at will. Then, we would all meet again for follow-up discussions, as we did tonight. Only next time it would be at the Steins' for dinner. After all that was settled and agreed to, the Steins departed, but not before Elaine loaded them down with food from the meal and a few cannoli, too. As they say, a good time was had by all, overall.

CHAPTER 8

JOE'S LETTER

I decided that I would write the following narrative for Bill and Liz. It is my attempt at a general overview of what Christians often refer to as end-time events. These key events, many Christians maintain, are what will signal the promised return of Jesus Christ to earth. When I had finished the narrative I sent it to Elaine, the high school English teacher, who edited it slightly, and then I sent it on to Bill and Liz. One thing is for sure, the next time we all meet there will be plenty to talk about regarding end-time events, and how they may impact Liz and Bill's planned move to Israel. Not to mention, their impact on Al, Elaine, me and the rest of mankind. Wow, our future discussions could get real heavy, real fast!

Dear Bill and Liz,

Here are seven major prophetic keys to end-time events, as this humble layperson understands them. Most traditional Christian scholars tie these events to the return of Christ, often referred to as the second coming. Additionally, I have footnoted key Scripture references, of both the Old and New Testaments. They are at the end of this email message. Together, they give us the prophetic predictions of end-time events. I also thought you might be interested in studying them, too, for yourselves.

1. Return of the Jewish people to the Land of Promise.

This happened in large numbers in 1948, with the establishment of the modern nation of Israel. It was a major fulfillment of what had been predicted centuries earlier in the Scriptures. It should also be pointed out that this was the third historical re-establishment, and also, that many Jews began migrating there much earlier than 1948. It started way back in the 1800s, when some German Lutherans moved there and continued on later in that century, with the formation of the Zionist movement. Having said all that, the fact remains that the major impetus for the establishment of the new nation was clearly World War II. Even more pointedly, it was Hitler's attempt at Jewish annihilation. The aftermath of that unimaginable nightmare resulted not only in the establishment of Israel, but it also created an even greater hunger for Jews to reunite in their ancestral home. Beyond that, it instilled a mighty fighting resolve in all Israelites to hold on to their homeland and modern identity, whatever the cost might be to do so.

Just a personal comment...it never ceases to amaze me how evil men try to thwart the plans of God, such as with the Nazis' diabolical Holocaust. Yet, inevitably, God turned their evil to his good purposes by re-establishing a modern Jewish nation in the ancient land of promise in 1948, only three years after the Nazis' slaughter of some six million Jews.

2. Most conservative theologians believe in a rapture, or the removal of all true believers in Christ from the earth, and that it will take place just prior to other major end-time events, including the second coming of Christ. These Christian scholars generally concur that there is no "prophetic" reason why this rapture could not happen at any time. However, in fairness, I must mention that although Elaine and I believe in a rapture and its happening prior to the second coming, not all serious Christians agree. Some think it happens after Christ's return and some think the second coming and the rapture are one and the same event. However, once it does happen, things will move rapidly, albeit over a period of time, which Christians refer to as the tribulation. The tribulation period will culminate with Christ's return with an army from heaven, which will defeat all the human armies arrayed against Israel. This defeat will take place at the well-known battle of Armageddon. After this defeat, Christ will rule the earth for a thousand years. This is known as his millennium reign.

3. Prior to Christ's return, the Jewish people, as we have previously noted, will have to once again go through great suffering.

The prophet Jeremiah called it "The Time of Jacob's Trouble." It will be greater than any other period of suffering, including the Holocaust. Except this time, the whole world will go through the suffering with Israel. It is the beginning of God's final judgment against a rebellious and unbelieving world.

4. Ironically, the final trigger setting off the time of Jacob's Trouble will actually be a peace treaty. This treaty will come at a time of great upheaval and turmoil in world events. It will seem like the whole world is out of control-and to a large degree that will be true. The peace treaty will be for seven years. It will be proposed by a most charismatic and highly regarded world leader, probably from a now powerful European federation of nations. Israel, facing the brink of destruction, will accept the treaty, since troops from north, east and south will be arrayed against her. By Israel's accepting the treaty, God's wrath is triggered and his final judgment begins to come upon Earth rapidly.

This political leader will also take on the role of the religious leader of a new one-world religious organization. Finally, he will seek to be worshipped in the rebuilt Temple. At that time, he will also reveal himself to be the anti-christ.

5. Shortly after the peace treaty is signed, Russia and Iran will break the peace treaty and attack Israel.

Many suggest that this will be Russia's way of challenging the growing power of the European federation. This federation, quite dependent on Middle Eastern oil, is now the West's only true super-power. The USA, now less dependent on Middle Eastern oil, and economically weakened by wars and global competition with Europe and China, is politically deeply divided. The geo-political consensus of her citizens leaning more towards a renewed isolationism from world affairs, than to her post-cold-war role as world policeman. The Russian and Iranian armies, who attack Israel first, will be miraculously turned back, mostly by catastrophic weather events, and eventually defeated. However, an even more formidable foe looms. A world army, gathered from Europe, the

Middle East, North Africa, and China, all under one world religious, political, and economic leader, begin to attack Israel with overwhelming superior force. Once again, their goal is to wipe out the entire nation of Israel. This is the acute beginning of "Jacob's Troubles." Jesus warned that when these things begin to happen, all Jews should flee from Jerusalem to the mountains.

6. With a massive and powerful army gathered against it, Israel will be backed into a corner, so to speak, at a place called Armageddon or Har Megiddo.

When things are at their bleakest point, Christ and the angelic armies from heaven will descend upon Israel. Christ will touch down upon the Mount of Olives, and in so doing will immediately change the geography of the plains of Megiddo, and also thereby shatter much of the opposing forces. Shortly thereafter, his army of angelic warriors will wage the final battle of Armageddon and defeat the vast but inferior human armies of the world.

7. Once Christ defeats both Satan's antichrist and the world army, he will set up a peaceful earthly kingdom for a thousand years.

This is known as the Millennium or the Millennial Kingdom of Christ's reign on earth as Lord of Lords and King of Kings. At the end of the Millennium, there is more that takes place, involving a final rebellion of Satan and those who still will not put faith in Christ; but for our purposes, we'll stop here.

There is certainly plenty of room for discussion about all that I have written. I look forward to our next time together and to that lamb dinner that you promised at your place.

Ciao for now,
Joe

Biblical footnotes:
Matthew 24:21, 25; Zechariah. 12:3; Luke 17: 26-30; Daniel 2, 7, 9; Revelation 6, 9, 12, 13,16, 17,18,19, 20; Joel 3; Isaiah 28; Ezekiel 38-39; Jeremiah 30.

CHAPTER 9

DINNER AT THE STEINS

Our schedules did not allow us to get together again until March 14.

As one might expect, the Steins had a beautiful and spacious home outside of the city in the historic town of Lexington. It was filled with beautiful furniture and paintings. Elaine was in awe as they showed us around the place. We marveled at their indoor swimming pool and sauna, as well as their weight room. I was reminding myself that, no matter how great their house was, Elaine and I had a mansion waiting for us in Heaven. After some soft drinks and light finger food in their spacious living room, we all sat down to a delicious lamb dinner, as promised. It was a great leg of lamb, with mint jelly, roasted potatoes, green bean casserole and all the fixings, as one might say. Elaine and I started to compliment Liz on being such a great cook, when to our surprise, she informed us that Bill is the chef in the family and, in fact, had done all of the cooking for the evening.

"Another great hidden talent of Billy Stein," I commented.

"It won't be hidden forever," Liz responded.

"Now what, another secret to be revealed?" Elaine asked.

"Well, when we get over to Israel, instead of practicing medicine, I hope to open up a small restaurant. It has always been a dream of mine, but it never seemed the right time or place in Boston," Bill explained.

"That's awesome!" Elaine and I seemed to say at the same time.

"Actually, we'll have a better idea this summer," Liz stated.

"Why is that?" asked Elaine.

"Al called the other day and we have been invited by the Israeli government to visit Israel to look at plans that the Knesset is developing for the Temple," Liz explained.

"The Knesset," Elaine asked, "that's the Jewish counterpart to our Congress, right?"

"Yes," Liz responded, "apparently they're deeply involved with this project, according to Al."

"That, I must say, does not come as any shock to us, given what we've been taught," I commented.

"That's fast moving and incredible. Do you have a date when

you're leaving on your trip?" I inquired.

"We go there exactly four months from tomorrow, March 15. So, we leave on July 15 and we plan to stay for two weeks to look around and scope out where we might want to live, along with meeting with Liz's government connections on the Temple project," Bill responded.

"Oh no, March 15 – beware the Ides of March!" blurted out the English teacher, jokingly.

Bill inquired with eyebrows raised, "Oh, come on now. That's not part of your end of times beliefs too, is it?"

"Of course not," Elaine quickly responded. "I just get caught up in my everyday work. Teaching *Julius Caesar* in one class and all the way over to *1984* in another class. I guess that I get programmed with it all."

Liz chuckled. "I guess you do. Wow, *1984.* We all read that back at Lane Polytech. Now, talk about a man who could see the future – that was George Orwell."

"Actually, it was Eric Blair," corrected Elaine.

"Who is Eric Blair?" asked Liz.

"That is George Orwell's real name."

We looked at each other and agreed that none of us ever knew that fact, save for Elaine.

"Whoever he really was, the guy kind of caught a real insight into the future. What with phrases that you hear tossed about in society today; such as, Big Brother is watching, the Thought Police, Groupthink, and Doublespeak," said Liz.

"You're absolutely right, and he was writing after World War II and got his work published in 1949 or about four decades prior to his forecasted date of 1984, when the world as we knew it would change forever. And in some ways he was clearly onto something," Elaine responded.

"To be honest with you, that is how I reacted when I read your email on the end of time events according to your Christian interpretation of the Bible. You may be on to something, or perhaps you are just good at creatively connecting the dots and coming to some very imaginative conclusions...not unlike George Orwell, err, Eric Blair," Bill stated.

"I see, so you think it just comes down to some creativity with connecting events from history and making up a good story out of the way we Christians interpret it in regard to the future?"

questioned Elaine.

"That's pretty much how I view it, too," said Liz. "*1984*, the book *Megatrends*, your end-times scenario-they are attempting to predict the future and to warn mankind and they all have grains of truth in them that should be seriously contemplated."

"For example?" I asked.

"For example," Liz responded, "when you talk about wars, earthquakes, famine, and Middle East tensions these things have been going on for centuries and certainly during the last two thousand plus years since Jesus Christ was on earth. To say that they are going to continue and get worse as time goes on, is no big, unusual conclusion that one could leap to, and with reasonable assurance of being correct to some degree."

"Come on, Joe," Bill countered. "With all due respect, you have to admit that to tell us that the second coming of a man that lived over two thousand years ago is based on the reality of more wars and natural disasters in the future, is pretty thin evidence."

"I see where you're coming from, and it's a commonly held perspective. However, what you are overlooking is that we are not talking about one or two prophetic utterances, by one or two people.

61

We also are not talking about predictions being made only a few decades prior to events, as with the works you mentioned. If we were, I would be more likely to agree with you. However, when — as a judge might say — you take a preponderance of the evidence, it's quite weighty in favor of the predicted second coming of Christ," I asserted.

Bill said, "Okay, be specific as to the preponderance of the weighty evidence and let Liz and I play judge and jury."

"You're on your honor, Your Honor; or is that you're on, Your Honor?" I asked jokingly, and we all laughed.

"Liz, you mentioned the book *Megatrends,*" Elaine, our well-read English teacher said. "In that work, did you know it was pointed out that over ninety percent of Americans believe in God, albeit with great religious diversity in the expression of that faith in a Supreme Being? That diversity has grown until today, we not only have the old, traditional denominations, but additionally all kinds of sects."

"So, what's your point?" asked Bill.

"I simply mention these facts because I think it is important to note, before we submit our evidence, that the vast majority of

Americans sense the work of a Supreme Being going on among them. And although many reject organized traditional religion, they are still seeking other ways and groups through which to connect with that Supreme Being in a way meaningful to their lives. Joe and I are part of that ninety percent and we believe we have found the way to connect to that Supreme Being through our faith in Christ as his Son and our Savior and Lord," Elaine boldly responded.

"*The* way to connect?" Bill quickly reacted.

"Of course, just as everyone else believes their faith system is the way for them. But it does go beyond that logic. It is common knowledge that Jesus said that he was 'the way' to know and commune with God by faith. That is why we believe it is so important for us, as believers of this teaching of Christ, to help all people discover it and moreover to discover it through faith in him," Elaine so nicely explained.

"So you see the books like *1984* as predictors of doom and gloom and that unless one is saved from their sins by Jesus Christ, life is pretty much a hopeless experience, is that it?" Liz asked.

"To be completely candid," Elaine explained, "that is how we view it. I like the way an old Christian saying puts it: 'Life without Christ brings one a hopeless end, while life with Christ brings one endless hope.' For us, there is much truth in that view of life."

"I for one, refuse to accept hopelessness as my world view, so I guess we will just have to agree to disagree on that point," Liz quickly stated.

"Sure, that's okay to agree to disagree, but before we close on the topic of hopelessness, I just want to make it very clear that Joe and I see great hope, not hopelessness," Elaine responded. Then she took out her final flash card and quoted her very favorite evangelical author, the famous Dr. Billy Graham.

Here is what Dr. Graham had to say on the topic of hope vs hopelessness,

"...there is hope for the future. God has planned utopia. There is a glorious new social order coming, but it is going to be brought by Jesus Christ Himself when He returns. I believe the time is short...listen to the voice of Jesus above the storm, say, ' So you also must be ready, because the Son of Man will come at an hour when you do not expect him." Citations 1.*Storm Warning*

"Wow, interesting and compelling thoughts; but again, only if you buy it, which we do not," opined Bill.

Then he tried to lighten up the mood a bit.

"When are Liz and I going to get to play judge and jury?"

"Right now," I said.

And then we started on our presentation on end-time predictions.

"You have already seen what the prophecy is foretelling in our recent email. So, now we will point out some of the facts behind those predictions," I started to explain.

"You may continue. But don't ask to approach the bar; we're all out of wine," Bill joked, then half apologized when Liz reminded him to take this seriously.

I continued, "The first and most concrete fact is the 1948 reestablishment of Israel and the subsequent re-gathering of her people. This was predicted at various times in the Old Testament."

"Fact number two is that knowledge shall increase and people will be running 'to and from,' according to Daniel the prophet's writings hundreds of years before Christ's first coming. Is there any doubt that this has come to pass? It took thousands of years for knowledge to double once, than about another hundred years for it to double again, then down to doubling in decades and now even more frequently than that. And with airline travel and other forms of modern transportation, people are traveling more and more within our 'global village,' to the point that we are just one small place connected by airports. This is changing the world and could it also be setting things up for a one-world government with one economy, and a one world-church, as Scripture also predicts will come about in the end times?"

Fact number three is the focus of the world: it is almost constantly being brought back to the Middle East and Israel. Regarding wars and rumors of wars, both Russia and the USA have both been involved in Middle-Eastern conflicts during the last few decades.

Israel today is constantly at risk because of the hatred towards her by her regional neighbors; such as Iran, Syria, Palestine, Egypt, and terrorist groups like Hamas. Hence, many believe that is where a nuclear war is most likely to break out in the world, which is exactly what the Scriptures predict in the battle of Armageddon, the battle that Christ returns to fight with his armies from heaven.

Fact number four --- and how could we forget this one, since we are living it presently is, the rebuilding of the Temple in Jerusalem. This is something Jesus predicted about two thousand years ago."

"There is just a bit more. Speaking of the Temple, I will never forget one of Al's talks on the subject at the store. In a way it ties in with your wonderful lamb dinner tonight, Bill."

"Really?" said Dr. Bill. "I've got to hear this one."

"One of the ways in which the Levi priests were ordained or set apart for their work was through the sacrifice of a lamb on the altar of the Temple," I said.

"I never knew that," said Liz.

"And I never did, either," said Elaine.

"Wasn't the tribe of Levi one of the original twelve Jewish tribes and the one from which all the priests of Israel were to come?" asked Bill.

"Absolutely correct," I responded. "When new Levi priests were to be set aside for their ministry among the people of Israel, a lamb would be slaughtered, then the blood of that lamb would be sprinkled on the new priests' ears, eyes, mouth, and feet. This was done as a reminder to the new priests to hear no evil, see no evil, speak no evil, and to not walk in any evil way. At least that's the basic idea, as Al explained it and I recall it."

"Al explained further," I said, "that after this was done, the people in attendance all ate the lamb that was slain on the altar, as part of their celebratory feast. So, that is one of the reasons that lamb is so popular in Jewish culture, as again evidenced by the wonderful lamb dinner that Bill prepared for us tonight."

"I do say, you're just full of good stuff for an old baseball player," Bill commented. "And to think, I was going to make chicken and dumplings."

At that, we all had a good laugh. Then Elaine re-focused us by saying,

"And to Christians, the Lamb of greatest importance was sacrificed on the cross of Calvary and his bloodshed to make atonement for our sins against a Holy God. That's why we call Jesus the Lamb of God. It all ties together so beautifully from Old Testament symbolism to New Testament fulfillment in Christ."

"And with that I will conclude our evidence presentation to the court. What say the judge and jury?" I asked.

"Well, after deliberating not at all and having only heard the evidence, my initial reaction is that although interesting, the evidence is inconclusive concerning the second coming of a man who lived two thousand years ago," said Bill.

"That is what I was thinking, and also that it is a matter of faith in these facts. I mean even if true, they do not necessarily prove a second coming of Christ," said Liz.

Elaine offered, "Actually, I tend to agree with both Liz and Bill, at least to this degree: there is no absolute proof in these predictions that Christ is coming again. It is really a matter of faith. However, at least it should be noted, that those of us who do believe that these events point to Christ's second coming, base it upon some real evidence, which has led us to a very reasoned conclusion. It is not just a, 'blind leap of faith.' "

"Oh, exactly." I said. "And our whole goal in these discussions is to not convince you of our belief's trustworthiness. It is an effort, in love, towards you two. We want you to see that if these things do begin to happen while you are living over there; that you would know what possibly to expect next."

"We understand," said Liz. "We appreciate all that you have shared with us and it does give one a lot to consider."

"Yes, said Bill. "And it certainly helps to better prepare us for the next major step in our lives."

"Okay then, let's just leave it at that for now. We certainly hope we can see you guys again during the spring and summer." I said.

"Absolutely" Bill said "Hey I have a great idea.

"Why don't we take in opening day at Fenway Park? It will probably be the last Sox opening day we will ever attend."

After briefly pausing and contemplating that heavy thought, Elaine inquired, "Oh that sounds like fun, but just what time of year is that?" Bill and I laughed as the ladies just looked at each other.

"It's always in early April." I chipped in.

"And the tickets will be on me," said Bill "I have some great connections with Dave Walker, the Sox ticket manager."

With that, the rest of the evening was filled with light hearted banter as we enjoyed the Steins' indoor heated pool. I don't think they will have this in Israel, I thought.

CHAPTER 10

GIRLS' NIGHT OUT

I got home late from work on Saturday, but it really didn't matter much, since Elaine was out all day with Liz as she did some shopping for Israel and then they had dinner together at the Nantucket Oyster Bar. The NOB, as locals like to refer to it, is a small place which concentrates on providing local produce, especially fresh fish. Its cooking is also strongly influenced by a New England fishermen's cuisine, combined with different cooking methods from all over the world. This gives the patrons offerings of differently spiced cooking. The NOB is an extremely popular place. It has a drop-in quality and a river view setting, which is thoughtfully decorated. This is where Elaine and I always try to sit. She and Liz were not able to sit there on their visit, but they enjoyed themselves nonetheless. And why not, it was a girls' night out evening, and they had a big trip to Israel to plan for and discuss.

We agreed ahead of time that I would hear all about it from Elaine on Sunday. So, I settled in for the evening, enjoying a quiet night alone- with my supper; pizza, chips and ice tea-followed by a great basketball game on local TV between the Chicago Bulls and the Celtics. The next morning Elaine and I headed off to Lexington Community Church, where we were long-time members. As we drove the twenty or so minutes to church, Elaine just began opening up about her day with Liz.

"Oh, I just don't know where to start," she started.

"Liz is such a wonderful person — bright, sociable, interesting, but, but..."

"But what?" I interrupted impatiently.

"But just so secular in her thinking," Elaine said, then continued...

"Even after all the sharing that you and I did with the Steins about our concerns, she was mostly interested in talking about my take on *1984,* by Orwell."

"I feel good that we at least told them what we believed and why. We told them what Israel is going to be facing, perhaps in our lifetime and perhaps it will be of help to Liz and Bill in their future, while living in Israel. Who knows? God does still work in mysterious ways," I offered.

"I know; and we kept our promise not to proselytize them,

but just to share; and I think — I know – we have honored that promise. Although..." Elaine trailed off.

"Although, what?" I asked.

"Maybe we need to share more of the gospel message of salvation with them," Elaine suggested.

"That is tricky, since we made that promise to them. However, if they ever ask us to explain our beliefs, then that would be our opportunity to share the good news of salvation through faith in Jesus Christ as the Messiah," I said.

"You're right, and I am sure that when they meet with Al over in Israel, he will share his faith in Christ with them. He is so bold about it, but..." said Elaine.

"But what?" I asked

"But, I already took that next step," said Elaine.

"You didn't!" I snapped back. "What specifically did you do?"

"I just gave her a notebook that I have been preparing for the Steins, with quotes and Bible verses and the prayer of salvation. That's all."

"That's all? How did she respond?" I asked anxiously.

"Oh, you know Liz. She was very gracious and accepted it in the spirit in which I offered, in love," said Elaine.

The conversation ended at that point, since we had arrived and were getting ready to enter church for the service. We then enjoyed, as always, another uplifting message from the pastor of this great church, Rev. Dr. David Arthur Lawton.

Elaine and I liked to visit Proiettos Bistro, another great Italian restaurant in the North End section of Boston, on Sundays and on most special occasions. At least it was either Proiettos Bistro or Davido's whenever we could afford it. To us, they were the two most authentic reflections of Italian dining Boston has to offer. And so it was that we decided to eat at Proiettos on this particular Sunday.

Almost immediately after we ordered, I turned the conversation back to Elaine's day with Liz. Elaine explained that Liz thought *1984* was so insightful and brilliantly written in predicting a lot of what we seem to be facing today, at least in general terms and she insisted on hearing Elaine's English teacher's view. So, Elaine took Liz through what she would essentially teach her senior AP English. Only instead of days, she condensed it down to one night over dinner. She gave Liz her perspective, which is that Orwell did do a brilliant job in warning us of the future. However, he did so in only general terms, not to be compared with the specific terms of the prophecies of the second coming of Christ. She also reminded Liz that *1984* only looks a few decades into the future, while the prophecy in the Old Testament was written around four hundred years prior to Christ's first coming. From there she just went on as she would with any other student, quoting from the noted author and humanist psychoanalyst, Erich Fromm. She said that Liz was intrigued by Fromm as well, especially after Elaine explained that he came from a family of Orthodox German Jews, a few of whom were accomplished Rabbinical scholars. However, Fromm rejected a good deal of his upbringing to embrace a more secular view of man. In this way, he came from a similar perspective as Orwell and of course as Liz and Bill Stein. During dinner, Elaine, always prepared like the good Girl Scout she once was, also gave Liz a handout that she often used in class. Essentially, it was an excerpt from Erich Fromm's critique of *1984* and Orwell in his Afterword:

The mood of hopelessness about the future of man   is in marked contrast to one of the most fundamental features of Western thought: the faith in human progress and in man's capacity to create a world of justice and peace. This hope has its roots both in Greek and in Roman thinking, as well as in the Messianic concept of the

Old Testament prophets. The Old Testament philosophy of history assumes that man grows and unfolds in history and eventually becomes what he potentially is. It assumes that he develops his powers of reason and love fully and thus is enabled to grasp the world, being one with his fellow man and nature at the same time preserving this individuality and his integrity. Universal peace and justice are the goals of man, and the prophets have faith that in spite of all errors and sins, eventually this "end of days" will arrive, symbolized by the figure of the Messiah.

What characterized Thomas More's Utopia, and all the others, is that they do not speak in general terms of principles, but give an imaginative picture of the concrete details of a society which corresponds to the deepest longings of man. In contrast to prophetic thought, these perfect societies are not at the end of the days, but exist already, though in a geographic distance rather than in the distance of time.

...the significance of Orwell's book is that it expresses the new mood of hopelessness which pervades our age, before the mood has become manifest and taken hold of the consciousness of people.

Orwell was not alone... Aldous Huxley, in *Brave New World* and the Russian author, Zamyatin in his book *We* have expressed attitudes and moods akin to Orwell's. These works contrast greatly with what one might call the positive trilogy: the Emerson, Thoreau and Whitman's writings of the 19th Century. As Fromm explains it:

 Ironically, between the negative and positive Utopias there was a dramatic societal shift away from old agrarian economics to the industrial age and all the scientific innovations of the emerging 20th century. In other words, when man can produce enough for everybody, when war has become unnecessary because technical progress can give any country more wealth than can territorial conquest, when this globe is in the process of becoming as unified as any continent was ...at the very moment when man is on the verge of realizing his hope, he begins to lose it..' This is an historical paradox.

Orwell... is not a prophet of disaster. He still hopes, but his hope is a desperate one. The hope can be realized only by recognizing...the dangers of a society...who will have lost every trace of individuality...and yet will not be aware of it.

76

While it is true that Orwell writes just after WWII and during the continued barbarism of the Stalinist Soviet System, his warnings are clearly for all of us in the West, too. Do we not sense... "Big Brother" is indeed watching us more than ever before? The question (in the 3 negative Utopias) is a philosophical, anthropological and psychological one and perhaps also a religious one. It is: can human nature be changed in such a way that man will forget his longing for freedom, for dignity, for integrity, for love...that is to say can man forget that he is human or does human nature have a dynamism which will react to the violation ...by attempting to change an inhuman society into a human one? 2. Citations, 1984 and Afterword

According to Elaine, Liz was taken by the fact that many of her secular beliefs were so well embodied by and expressed by so many, including Orwell, Huxley, and Fromm, a fellow secular Jew. She then ended the evening by trying to lovingly remind Liz that it was also her great Jewish ancestors of faith who gave us the prophecies about a Jew called Jesus, the Christ. With that being said, Elaine, rather boldly for her, gave Liz another item, a three-ring binder notebook, full of various pieces of information about Christ, the second coming, and topics related to it.*

She had spent weeks compiling it. She told Liz that she hoped that she would accept it in the spirit in which it was given, one of love and concern and not of one trying to win an argument. Liz seemed to be okay about it, according to Elaine. And at least

Elaine felt that she had done all she could in this regard as our dear friends were preparing for their move to Israel.

Elaine further explained to Liz that, in contrast to Orwell, a number of these items reflected established facts of history, many of which had been predicted by members of the Steins' own Jewish heritage, several hundred years before Christ. Then Elaine continued talking to me about her feelings in regard to all her efforts of putting these lists and verses together for the Steins.*

"In the end, I don't know if any of it will sink in, since both Liz and Bill have such a secular orientation and everything we believe seems so far out there for them to ever really reason through," commented Elaine.

*Appendices, Item A, Elaine's Notebook

CHAPTER 11

ISRAEL ANYONE?

The big day finally came and was it ever a big one! Opening day at Fenway Park, our beloved Boston Red Sox vs. the Chicago White Sox. Since the game didn't start until 1 pm, the four of us got together for brunch at Natasha and Nitsa's Golden Boys' Diner, right across from Fenway. Natasha was Japanese-American and her life-long friend Nitsa, a lovely Greek women, was married to Natasha's brother Danny. Danny managed the restaurant, while his cousin Jonathan was its lead cook. It was a real family affair. The ladies were warm and gracious hostesses as were all their veteran wait staff: Brenda, Sue, Peggi, KB, Diane, Anita, Patti, Rosie, Ruth, Riki, Stacy and Mary. Their regular customers, like us, loved them all. Hence, most customers were regulars except on game days. The N and N girls, as they were lovingly called, greeted us warmly and led us to our table. We felt comfortable immediately.

However, today we naturally wanted to hear all about the Steins' upcoming trip to Israel and that is truly all that Liz and Bill wanted to talk about. They had great pictures with them, sent by the

Israeli government via Al Hoffman. So, first they talked about Al Hoffman and the fact that he was now a believer in Jesus or as Al would call him, Yeshua Mashiach, a zealous Messianic Jew, and that he seemed ever so happy to be living in the homeland of his ancestors.

"But you already knew that about Al, didn't you?" asked Bill.

"Yes, sure, but Al made us promise not to go into it with you two. I guess he was afraid you might not take the trip, if you knew ahead of time," I jokingly answered.

"We understand, but wow, you may not have tried to convert us, but that Al sure is doing all he can," Bill said. "He sent us pictures of all the holy sites, with Scriptures and explanations attached to each one as to how they related to Yeshua. He sent us these," Bill continued, as he showed the pictures Al had sent. They were the place of the cross, the Garden of Gethsemane, the burial tomb, and Bethlehem.

"But, then he sent us flyers about his Messianic Church and well, you get the big picture-conversion city ahead."

"You're being a bit too critical," Liz admonished. "Al is just trying to share his faith passion with us. Underneath, he is still the

80

same old Al, loving, full of fun and very thoughtful."

"As a believer, I would love to see all those places," said Elaine.

"Well, you both will just have to visit us once we're settled, or better still, why don't you just come with us in July? Elaine will be out of school, and couldn't Hugo run the store for a couple of weeks? It would add so much to the experience if you were there and...," said Liz.

"Wow! Now Liz, I do not know if we could pull off those kinds of plans in such a short time frame... and the money. I mean we're doing okay at present; but what about Mr. Bill, he may not want us tagging along, or Al, for that matter," I responded.

"I wouldn't mind one bit. I am with Liz on this one. I think it would be a super idea. What do you think Elaine?" Bill asked.

"I don't know," said Elaine. "Like Joe said, it would be expensive and there would be a lot to plan and, well, maybe we just need to pray about it and think it through a bit," Elaine said.

"There you go, we'll pray about it," I said.

We ended our conversation on that note and then briefly focused on their response to Al's initiative with the pictures and Al's explanations and all he had sent them.

"Al's pictures were quite impressive and I must admit, I am much more open to the fact that Jesus may be who he claimed to be, the Son of God," said Liz.

"Open, but not convinced?" I asked.

"I guess that's about right," Liz went on to say.

"And how about you, Doctor?" I asked.

"No, it was all very nice seeing the pictures and hearing the story as Al laid it out for us with each picture, but to be honest with you, the idea of God coming to earth, taking on human form and dying on a cross and then rising from the dead-it's just all too far out there for me-too much like science fiction and not enough like science for this old skeptic." Bill responded.

"Hey, at least you're being honest and we appreciate and respect that totally," I commented.

"Al did insist on one thing. In one of his lengthy emails, he had to make sure we knew how to become, "saved," as he put it, in case we decided to commit our lives to Jesus," Liz added.

"He even had a name for it, he called it the..." said Bill.

"The sinners' prayer," Elaine interrupted.

"Right, I should have known you two would know it," Bill finished.

"That and the fact that I put Billy Graham's version of it in the notebook that I gave to Liz," said Elaine.

"Let's see," said Liz," 'Dear God, I am a sinner and I now ask Jesus to come into my life and cleanse me of my sin and be my Lord and Savior."

"Or words to that effect," said Bill.

"Words to that effect is exactly right, Bill. It really isn't the words that count, as much as the sincere expression of faith behind them. God knows what we mean. And much more importantly, he knows our hearts," I responded.

"No, we get it. We just don't believe it," Bill reminded us.

"I just told Al that if we ever changed our minds and hearts, we would just contact him or you two." Liz added.

Then Liz went on to explain how Al insisted we know the prayer, because he or we might not always be around and not just because of death. Then he gave them his thoughts on a "rapture" of all true believers, who would be gone in an instant. We recalled how we had also tried to explain to them that many serious Christians

83

maintain that there will be a time, prior to Jesus' second coming when he will take his church to be with him and that this could happen at any time and that it would happen quickly. In that eventuality, they would only have the sinners' prayer to go by. There would be no believers to turn to after the rapture, except new believers. So, the prayer, along with any Bible verses they might know of, may prove their only guide to putting their faith in Jesus. At that point, Bill and Liz didn't seem comfortable discussing the rapture any further. So, the balance of the time was spent looking at pictures and hearing about the business aspects of their upcoming trip. Apparently, Bill will try to look for spots to locate his restaurant and Liz will meet with members of the planning committee for the rebuilding of the Temple. She may even get to see some preliminary plans. Also, they hope to look at some places to live.

In the process, Liz confirmed two important facts to us. First, that according to Al, the committee was planning to build on the grounds of the original site, but perhaps about one hundred or so yards away from the Dome of the Rock Mosque; and second, they were planning to have a section for animal sacrifices, to accommodate those Jews looking for a return to the old Mosaic

Laws, which include animal sacrifices. To Elaine and me, those were amazing revelations, because they were predicted as part of end-times prophecy thousands of years ago.

Finally, we made it over to Fenway and settled in for the game. Elaine and I had lived in the Boston area our whole lives and had never been to an opening day at Fenway. And now, there we were, sitting in beautiful seats along the first base line. All compliments of Dr. Billy Stein. We had a great time watching the opening ceremony featuring an Army color guard, the Blue Angels flying over, and the crowd, singing "The Star Spangled Banner." The crowd also sang "Take Me Out to the Ball Game," "Carolina," and "God Bless America" at various times during the game. We also enjoyed eating popcorn, Fenway Franks, hot dogs and big bags of peanuts. To us, the highlight of it all, besides watching the Red Sox win the game, was watching them get their rings for winning the World Series the year before. Our guys were the World Champions once again, and we all were feeling the passion of being Boston Strong. Of course, we also had to put up with Billy downing several beers and thereby getting a bit loud and silly. And as the ex-jock in the group, I had to, of course, do an analysis for all of us.

"They never should have left Brewster in so long. He was getting hit hard by the third inning," I commentated.

"I don't think the manager has much confidence in his bullpen," Bill opined.

Liz picked up on that one. "Bullpen, I thought we were at a baseball game, not a bull fight. What the heck is a bullpen?"

We all laughed, but then we realized she was serious, so we spent the next fifteen minutes trying to explain to Liz what a bull pen was, in baseball parlance.

In any event, I finally finished my analysis, but not until we were walking out of Fenway.

"I think in the nine-inning game, the Sox proved to me that they are going to be strong in power hitting (final score, 8-5, with 3 home runs), defense (0 errors) and hitting (13 hits total), but their pitching needs to come around and the relief out of the bullpen, or it could be a long season."

Bill interrupted and responded,

"Blah, blah, blah. And so what else is new with the Red Sox? New season, same results, they're awesome and their uniforms and Fenway both look great, too!"

We certainly had a terrific day at the old ball park with our dear friends.

In fact, we had such a good time that we got together several more times over that baseball season at Fenway and the Red Sox won all those games. Liz seemed often fixated on watching the guys in the bullpen. As for Elaine, she just was happy to be there eating her peanuts and hot dogs. She also cheered the loudest when the Sox did something positive.

In addition, we did other fun things together. As history buffs, we took a day to go strolling along the Freedom Trail and seeing its many historic places. We also spent some summer times at the fountains in the Rose F. Kennedy Greenway; a knit-together group of parks, Fort Independence, which offers free tours and Castle Island, with hamburgers and hot dogs for under two bucks. One afternoon, we even climbed the Bunker Hill Monument, where the first major battle of the American Revolution was fought. When Elaine was teaching about the battle, she would always tease her students with, "Now just remember students, the Battle of Bunker Hill wasn't fought on the level." She said the kids always laughed, but we just groaned. Although, maybe it had something to do with

87

the fact that we were also now climbing up this hill and getting quite the workout from it. I can't imagine how they did it with all that gear on during the heat of the battle. Later on the very same day we visited the warship, Old Ironsides. It is the oldest commissioned ship in our Navy. It goes out to sea a short distance twice a year, or so we were told.

Our outings also took us to places like the John F. Kennedy Library, the Museum of Science and the Boston Aquarium. We also did some boating, golfing and tennis. The bond between us was growing deeper, but of course the time we had was also growing shorter. The planning committee wanted Liz to join them sooner than in the New Year, so the Steins were beginning to adjust their moving schedule. Besides, there wasn't much to hold them here.

Bill's practice was now closed and all his patients reassigned and Liz finished her last project at Andrews-Passeroni Associates in April. Their home and investment properties were now gone as well. In fact they had been staying in a nice hotel since the first of June.

CHAPTER 12

THE MORETTIS' BIG DECISION

It was a beautiful June Day and since Elaine had no school, we decided to play a round of golf with Bill and Liz at Triggs Golf Course, in Providence, R.I. It is a great course for occasional golfers, as well as challenging enough for expert golfers, such as the Steins. Bill also liked Triggs because the head of grounds' maintenance was non-other than his old college buddy from Brown University in Providence, one Howie Elton King.

"Yeah, Howie is a serious Christian, and a deacon in his Baptist church," Bill pointed out. Howie caught up with us at the first tee, along with his all white, blue-eyed Siberian husky pal, Suka. These two were inseparable and had been for years. He was so proud of that dog. So, we petted Suka, even as we chattered with Howie. After a brief chat, Al had to get back to his work. Before walking off, Howie said, "Be sure to stop by the Trigg's Restaurant. We call it the *19th Hole*. I'll try to catch up with you there. But, no matter, lunch is on my tab." "What a nice guy!" I commented. "That's Howie," said Bill. "Always kind, thoughtful and generous."

89

Since Liz and Bill were seasoned golfers, we paired off as teams of gals and guys. You guessed it, we played a full eighteen holes and the ladies beat us by three strokes. So, being the gentlemen that we are, we took them to lunch at the *19th Hole*-on Howie King. Howie stopped by and was put into a mild state of shock when Bill told him that he and Liz were soon moving to Israel. "You have got to be kidding me," said Howie. "Why, When?" "I sure wish we had stayed in better touch in recent years." "Oh, Howie. You will just have to come and visit us sometime, that's all." "Well, you know," said Howie. "I am on the Mission's Committee at my church and we do support a missionary work in Jerusalem." "Really, is it Shemar Y'Isarel, by any chance?" Elaine inquired. "Why, yes it is," said Howie. Then we all shouted in unison to him, "Al Hoffman!" "Yes, Al Hoffman is the guy I often correspond with for our church." "What a small world," Liz commented.

Then we all tried to excitedly explain the connections we all had to Al, but Howie had to get back to work soon. So, we exchanged numbers and email addresses with Howie and then we promised to tell Al and to keep in touch with him. In turn, Howie, promised to start praying and planning for a trip to Israel someday.

After, Howie left the table, the talk turned to the big elephant in the room. The question of whether the Morettis were going to Israel with the Steins on their visit to Israel. You should have seen the reaction when Elaine and I said that we had decided to go with them.

I thought that Liz was going to lose her ice cream cone, she was so excited. "Oh, how fantastic!" Liz exclaimed.

Then the Steins surprised us with some more good news. They said that since the Israeli government was paying for their trip to Israel, they would pick up half the tab for us. We tried to argue, but they insisted that this is what they wanted to bless us with. What a pair of great people!

"We'll have to start planning the details ASAP," Liz said to Elaine.

"Of course," said Elaine. "How about over lunch at Davido's next Saturday? After lunch, the two of us can go shopping for the trip."

Bill and I knew what that meant. We just needed to work out the details of the travel arrangements and leave the shopping and packing to the wives, which was fine with us.

CHAPTER 13

YESTERDAY BOSTON, TODAY TEL AVIV

We landed at Ben Gurion Airport, near Tel Aviv, Israel's capital, on July 10 around 8 am their time. If we thought we were experiencing Israeli culture on the flight over, we were hit with realities even stronger as we made our way through security at the airport. Al had warned us what to prepare for, but as with most reality versus imagination experiences, the real thing still shook us up a bit. As one might expect, Israel takes their security very seriously and it is nothing like one would experience at customs in the USA or Europe. The questions were quite personal, and the stern demeanor of the questioner was unsettling. In addition, there were Israeli soldiers in each corner of the room, armed with machine guns. They asked about our itinerary, how we packed and what we packed in our luggage. Then they focused in on why we wanted to travel in Israel. It took a long time and I thought we were never going to get out of there. But once we finally made it through and got to the baggage area, right there to greet us was our dear old friend Al Hoffman, formerly of Boston and now a proud dual citizen of Israel

92

and the USA. Al was right on time to pick us up and drive us to our hotel. It was so great to see him again and the hugs and kisses showed it. He looked terrific and you could tell that life in Israel was agreeing with him. As we drove off to our hotel, we told Al about the heavy questioning at the airport. Al just gently reminded us that they do it to protect us, not to harm us, and that patience is the key. He was, of course, right on both counts. It might have been morning, Israeli time, but it was night to us and we were exhausted from a long flight. So we made plans to see Al for lunch the next day and said, "good-night," at around 11 am, Tel Aviv time.

But tonight would be ours to enjoy. And enjoy we did! Tel Aviv is a city that is alive and vibrant. We had dinner in a delightful upscale restaurant in the Tel Aviv Port area of the city. Then it was on to the long promenade boardwalk to watch the sun set into the Mediterranean on this beautiful summer night. Elaine and Liz especially enjoyed browsing at the trendy little shops at the Pedestrian Mall, as they term it, or officially The Nahalat-Binyamin. It is just a wonderful little couple of streets of stalls offering a medley of handmade items, such as pottery and jewelry. All at reasonable prices, or at least that's what Elaine and Liz tried to convince Bill and me of as they purchased several pieces of "memories," as they referred to them. All in all, our first night in Israel was truly one of making and buying "memories."

We finished off the night with some dancing in the Neveh-Tredek district. We danced at an upscale club adjacent to an orange tree-lined and spectacularly lit square that I can only describe as magical. Elaine and Liz thought it a very romantic place, so it was easy for Bill and me to be their heroes that night. However, I was so tired from the flight and time change that I tripped over Elaine and myself several times. And Bill, ever present with his picture taking and video making, was capturing it all, especially my awkward dancing. By day we could verify that Tel Aviv was a great cultural center, but by night we could definitely experience and understand why it is the entertainment center of Israel, as well.

We slept in a bit late the next morning. Then Al picked us up and drove us to a great little café for lunch in the Carmel Market neighborhood. It had outstanding modern Israeli cuisine and Al proclaimed it one of his favorite eating places. Who could argue with dear Al, especially when he picked up the tab, too? Then, as planned, he and Liz had to head over to a meeting with the Israeli

Interior Department to discuss the Temple project.

While they were gone, Bill, Elaine and I decided to explore Tel Aviv on foot. Actually, we found it to be a great way to explore, because of the relative smallness of this capital city, coupled with the fact that its landscape is flat. The city has only four main arteries, all running parallel to the Mediterranean Sea. So we walked up one street and down another for the bulk of the afternoon. It was needed exercise as well, after all the great food we'd been eating. Of course we stopped along the way to visit the points of interests, such as the beachfront promenade, Center City, and Jaffa, where a certain man named Jonah was swallowed by a big fish-or whale, if you prefer. Jaffa was a hit with all three of us and we wished only that Liz was with us to enjoy it. Later we told her of our day and it seems that the flea markets, boutiques, and trendy restaurants were our consensus favorites. Jaffa, one of the earliest seaports known to man, had certainly come a long way since Jonah's day. Of course we were also anxious to hear about Liz's afternoon meeting. This catching up on our day took place over another spectacular meal at one of Al's other favorite Tel Aviv places, Café Bauhaus. Actually, I think he picked it because of Liz, because Bauhaus is actually a type of architecture that emphasizes white. In fact, Tel Aviv is often called the white city, because of the predominance of Bauhaus buildings. I knew all this because of my trusty tour book from Triple AAA that I read from cover to cover on the plane coming over. Another thing about that plane ride on El Al is the fact that from the moment we left New York, we began to experience the culture of Israel; from the security to the food, we knew that we were a minority in the midst of a predominantly Israeli group of passengers and of course, staff. Though a bit different, the flight was an enjoyable experience. Tel Aviv could also be called the Café City, because cafés are nestled throughout the city and are run by very inventive chefs. In fact, to call many of these establishments, cafés can also be a bit misleading, since many of them are really world-class restaurants, especially in their cuisine. It is hard to get a bad meal in this, "city that never sleeps," as it is also known. The attraction at this high-end café was that its seafood, and some other items, were flown in from around the world: lobster from Maine, purple colored rice from China, wild berries from Holland, clams from France, and snapper from New Zealand, to name just a few. Elaine and Liz both enjoyed their crispy calamari and Greek Salads with big chunks of feta drizzled with olive oil. The three guys all chowed down on chicken and lamb kabobs. However, all five of us also had a Middle Eastern favorite, Majadarah, which is rice and lentils, served along with salad and yogurt.

"Boy, I'll tell you one thing," said Bill. "I could never open up a restaurant in Tel Aviv. The competition would be overwhelmingly superior to what I could put out. This is superb food."

We all generally agreed, but by far, the most fascinating topic that evening was Liz's meeting. She and Al told us that they wanted the Steins to move to Jerusalem sooner rather than later and for Liz to spearhead the architectural part of the project.

"How amazing is that?" Al asked. We all concurred. Al was to be the government's official liaison host for the Steins as well. This meant that he would help them through the transition to their new homeland and Liz's new job. That was a comforting thought to both Bill and Liz, but the idea of the overall move and new work appeared quite daunting.

"Boy, we have a lot to talk about honey," Bill said to Liz.

"Yeah, and a whole lot to think about," Liz responded.

"And a whole lot to pray about," Al reminded us.

For now, though, all we wanted to do was get back to the hotel and sleep on it.

CHAPTER 14

ON TO JERUSALEM

The next morning we checked out of our hotel, packed up Al's van and headed from Tel Aviv down to Jerusalem. We drove out of Tel Aviv and down past the fashionable seafront of sun-soaked beaches. One after another, we drove by Bograshov Beach, the most crowded beach, and Sheraton "separated" Beach, where the genders must swim separately for religious reasons.

"Yay!" commented Liz, "and no doubt so that the women don't have to be bothered by some annoying overly zealous Israeli men."

Elaine had already gotten a taste of what that was like when strolling through the streets of Tel Aviv.

"I always thought you Italians were a bit too friendly with all your hugging and kissing," Elaine said to me," but these Jewish guys take a back seat to no one."

In any event, next it was Caesarea Beach which had ruins of the Roman and Crusade periods as its setting.

"Just can't get away from your Roman ancestors, even here

99

where my people live," Bill joked.

And, yes of course, we just had to stop for more pictures, especially by Billy, the great photographer.

Finally we journeyed by Coral Beach as we left Tel Aviv behind. Coral Beach is where a lot of the divers go to view coral formations. So, it was quite a diverse group of beaches that we beheld along the shore highway. The highway drive to Jerusalem was less than an hour down their scenic Route 1 and the beaches made it a most enjoyable journey.

We arrived at our hotel, The Grand Plaza, in West Jerusalem around 11 am, registered and went to our rooms. Then we met Al again at 1 pm for lunch. We decided to just relax and eat a light lunch at one of the Grand Plaza hotel restaurants. The Grand Plaza was going to be our home for the next week, plus. So, we were anxious to settle in and get to know it. We met in the Scala Restaurant, located at the top of the hotel. We enjoyed the meal, but soon realized that this was not the outstanding fare that we had enjoyed in Tel Aviv. Yet, there was a quiet elegance to this restaurant and our hostess, Mea, was delightful. Al told us that although West Jerusalem was known for the Cultural Mile running through it, it was not well regarded for its restaurants. There were only a few really quality ones in the area.

"That's actually good news to me," Bill commented. "This sounds like the type of area I could open up a café in and compete well."

"You're right, Honey," agreed Liz.

"Except, most everything in West Jerusalem is kosher, save for the café at the YMCA, for obvious reasons," Al added.

"The first thing is to find a location," said Bill, "so I would like to get some ideas at least, on this trip, if possible."

"Sure," said Liz, "so maybe you guys could scout out the area while I'm at work, but we also have to find a place or at least an area to live in, too, for when we move here."

"Sounds like a lot to do in a short time," Elaine remarked.

"Oh no, this will be fun," said Al. "And, I am at your disposal every day that you want me to drive you around. I am very familiar with this area as well. In fact I will start by showing you where I live and where my church is, if that's okay?"

We all agreed to follow Al, our "tour guide." Hence, we did that "religiously," for days.

CHAPTER 15

AL'S ISRAELI NEIGHBORHOOD

Al first took us to his Reshavia neighborhood, centrally located near downtown. We parked outside of Al's condo and began a stroll of the area from there.

As Al explained, "You are going to experience the hustle and bustle of city life here. However, in Jerusalem you need to understand that it is more about being centrally located, where public transportation is available, than it is about spacious suburban living, like one might find back home."

"Coming from Boston, that will not be a major adjustment," said Liz.

"I thought the same thing when I came over and it is no doubt true. City living is city living," said Al.

"True enough, but Liz and I lived out in Lexington, which was not as much city lifestyle as Boston. Is there something comparable we can look at here?" Bill asked.

"Comparable, I do not know, but hopefully close enough. I will show you that kind of area. I also have a friend from church,

Pam Johnson Rosenbaum, who is a realtor. She has offered to show you some places, too," Al responded.

"Oh, a friend from church. How close a friend?" Bill kiddingly inquired.

"No Bill, She is just a friend. Pam is a pretty Swedish lady, very bright, very Christian, and also very happily married to a messianic Jewish insurance agent named Paul Douglas Rosenbaum. They moved here from Providence, R.I. fifteen years ago. As a matter of fact, I think that you have a friend in common," Al remarked.

"Are you talking about Howie King?" Bill asked.

"That would be it," said Al. "Howie comes over here every couple of years as the missionary liaison from his home church back in Rhode Island. They are very supportive of our messianic church ministry here."

"See, Honey,'' said Liz. "Howie's visits Al, the Rosenbaums are from Providence, and who knows what others from back home are now living here. So, you're going to transition faster here than you think."

Just then we passed Falafels, set in a little kiosk-type

building. These little food kiosks are very different from an American fast food joint, such as McDonalds. Although, you will also find real McDonalds in this city. Al insisted that we stop at a kiosk. He pointed out that even though we would wait in line for our "fast food," the wait would be worth it, and he was absolutely right. We enjoyed samplings of sabich, a pita stuffed with lamb, fried eggplant and hard boiled eggs, and shwarma, which is a grilled turkey, also served on pita bread. Al commented that these little kiosks are nestled all around Jerusalem, but a tourist might never notice them because all the signs are in Hebrew.

Elaine and I were just looking at each other as if we were along for the ride in the middle of a dream, or so it seemed to us. And we hadn't even visited one of the holy sites yet.

"Bill," I said, "you could start with one of these little kiosks."

"Brewing coffee and waiting on long lines all day? I don't think so. It would be profitable, but a bit too much like running a hybrid, sort of a Hebrew McDonald's," Bill responded.

We all had a good laugh imagining Bill's idea of a kiosk as a Hebrew McDonald's.

Al quipped, "At least you figured out that it is biblical to

104

have men brew the coffee in Israel."

"Whatever are you talking about?" Bill asked.

"Well you noted what it says in the Bible...he brews, he brews," Al tweaked Bill.

"Too funny," said Liz.

Even though it was so silly, we all couldn't help but chuckle, before moving on.

Next, Al took us by his Messianic church, snuggled right in the heart of downtown and only a few blocks from his condo.

It was a small, but very interesting place, unlike anything I had ever seen. There wasn't anything quite like it back home. It was a complete blend of Jewish traditional items in a contemporary Protestant Church setting.

Liz found a brochure on a small table near the entrance to the sanctuary. It had colorful pictures, with accompanying text. It detailed the church's vision and beliefs. (refer to Appendix D)

After scanning the pages, Liz remarked, "They are pretty straightforward telling what they are all about."

Al then continued to inform us, "The Messianic Jewish movement is very active in Israeli politics, generally supporting the center-right coalitions and leaders. Hence, they are actively sought after and cultivated by the politicians who seek their vote and their money. This relationship, as we Americans know so well, develops influence for the group, which in this case is the Messianic Jewish community."

"It sounds like politicians are pretty much the same all over the world," Elaine commented.

"Yes, at least in the democratic countries," I pointed out.

"That's correct, and the truth be told, that influence has brought about the participation of some Messianic Jews at the very highest levels of the Israeli government. Yet, Messianic Jews only comprise a small portion of the international Jewish community," Explained Al. Then Al went on, "At a recent gathering of the World Congress of Jewish Studies, the very first panel focused on the role and influence of Messianic Jews and they generally concluded that believers in "Yeshua" (Jesus) and the Messianic Jewish movement worldwide are a significant phenomenon."

Al concluded his remarks by informing us of the following facts:

> That generally speaking, Christians have become Israel's best

friends and tourism has developed a love for the land of Israel among Christians living all around the world.

> That during times of turmoil and world crisis, many people turn to the Bible in order to understand the role of Israel in world events.

> That today the international news outlets each have offices in Israel, demonstrating the importance of activities there for the future of the world.

CHAPTER 16

CHANUKAH AND CHRISTMAS

As we continued to look around the church, Al explained how his Messianic church celebrates both Chanukah and Christmas each year, because of the way the two holidays are tied together. Rather than just his own explanation, Al gave us each a tract that contained his Pastor's sermon on the topic.

Then he introduced it by saying, "Each year Christians celebrate Christmas with children's pageants, carols, and gift exchanges. By the same token, Jewish people light candles, spin dreidles and open small gifts during the eight days of Chanukah. But what most Christians and Jews don't seem to realize is that there would have been no Christmas if it weren't for Chanukah."

Here's how Al's senior Pastor, Rabbi Dr. Paul Everett Fischer explained it in a sermon that the church printed out.

"Chanukah commemorates the courageous uprising of the Jews against the Syrians, the guerrilla war they waged to reclaim their religious freedom, and the great victory they enjoyed as a result of God's miraculous intervention.

The struggle began around 170 B.C., when the Syrian-Greek king Antiochus Epiphanes ruled over Israel. Wanting a unified empire, he imposed Greek culture on all the nations he ruled. In Jerusalem, he erected a statue of the Greek god Zeus in the Temple courts and commanded the Israelites to worship it. Pagan altars were erected throughout Israel and the Jewish people were forced to use them to sacrifice pigs, which God called unclean. The penalty for disobedience was death. Bible study, keeping the Sabbath, circumcision, and celebrating holy days as commanded in the Bible were forbidden. The Syrians also sacrificed a pig to Zeus on an altar they built on top of the Temple altar of burnt offering.

A Levitical priest named Mattathias moved with his family from Jerusalem to the small town of Modiâ to escape the persecution. When the king's officers tried to make Mattathias offer a pagan sacrifice, he refused and fled to the wilderness. Others joined him, forming an army that became known as the Maccabees. For three years, this ragtag band of farmers fought against the mighty Syrian army and achieved amazing victories through God's grace.

Finally the Maccabees launched a surprise attack, recapturing Jerusalem and the Temple. They cleansed the Temple, and three years to the day after the Syrians had profaned it, rededicated it to the Lord with great joy. It was also decided that this re-dedication should be observed every year as the Festival of Dedication, or Chanukah.

Today, Chanukah is celebrated by lighting candles in an eight-branched menorah each evening to remember God's miracle with the Temple oil. When the Maccabees regained control of the Temple, they found enough oil to light its Great Menorah for only one day, and, according to the Law of Moses, eight days were required to consecrate more oil. However, God made this little bit of oil last eight days until more could be prepared.

Looking at history through a spiritual lens, the Maccabees victory had a significant effect. Defeat would have meant the end of Biblical Judaism and the Jewish peoples' assimilation into Greek culture. If that had happened, Yeshua (Jesus Hebrew name) could not have come as the Messiah. He could only come to an Israel that lived according to the Law of Moses, so he could redeem mankind as the sinless Lamb who had not broken the Law. Therefore Chanukah should be celebrated by everyone who appreciates the coming of Yeshua." 3. Citations, Website quotation.

"I never knew about those two holidays tying together historically and spiritually like that." said Elaine.

"Neither did I," I offered.

"Well, we sure didn't," Bill said.

"I had no clue, said Liz. That is truly amazing, when you know all the history."

After visiting the church, we walked to see Al's condo. It was modest, but nicely furnished, not quite a bachelor pad, and certainly not a man-cave, but let's just say it had the male lived-in look. Actually, the first impression of an Israeli condo kind of encouraged Liz, she would tell us later.

She found it bigger and more modern than she had expected. She just wondered if she could deal with so much of the city noise right outside her window. Bill later said he would be happy in a place like Al's if he could just walk to work. And if not, he preferred a more suburban setting.

Al, ever the gracious host, served coffee and cake. We relaxed for a while as we discussed our plans for the next few days. Some two hours later, Al loaded us in his van and proceeded to give us a brief driving tour as we took the long way back to the hotel. We passed by Ben Yehuda and Jaffa streets, which form an open-air pedestrian mall; and the Moshava or German colony, established by breakaway Lutherans in the late 1800s. One can still see German inscriptions on many of the houses. Al pointed out to us that this group actually thought they could somehow hasten the second coming of Christ by moving to the Holy Land.

CHAPTER 17

AL'S MESSIANIC JUDAISM

This morning, we gathered for breakfast around 9 am in another restaurant of the Grand Plaza, Alan and Gracie's American Grille. "Go figure," I remembering saying to Elaine as we entered.

We no sooner had ordered our meals, when Bill started a heavy conversation right up again.

"Al, I still don't get what your Messianic Judaism is all about. Mixing Judaism and Christianity seems to me like another needless hybrid, only a religious one. Why don't people just stick to their own religious heritages?" asked Bill.

"Sometimes we love our heritage, but have been further enlightened by something or someone who comes later, like Jesus and Christianity. We view Christianity as an extension of Judaism, albeit with some major modifications," Al responded.

"I get it," said Liz. It's just like you and me Bill. We love our ethnic Jewish heritage, but really live by secular ideas that do not include God at all."

"That's an interesting way of looking at it," said Elaine.

We all concurred. Then Al pointed out more facts about Messianic Judaism in Israel. From brochures his congregation published, we learned even more facts.

"At the foundation of the State of Israel in 1948 there were but a handful of Israeli Jews who believed that Jesus is the Messiah...The movement experienced substantial growth in the 1990s. By the turn of the millennium, leaders of the movement estimate that there were between 5,000 and 7,000 Messianic believers scattered in some eighty congregations and house fellowships throughout the land of Israel. These figures include Gentiles either married to Jewish believers or who feel solidarity with the movement."
4. Citation, Casparini Center

Al said, "Today it is estimated that there are about 150 Messianic congregations around Israel. Their worship meetings are in different languages because, of course, they migrated from various countries to Israel. That is quite an expansion, since the estimated 20,000 Messianic Jews in Israel today grew from 1948 when only 12 Jews who believed in Jesus could be counted. They were counted in 1987 at 3,000 and in 1997 at 5,000."

Al proceeded to explain. "There is increasing tension between the now estimated 20,000 Messianic Jews, who nonetheless still consider themselves to be Jews ethnically, and orthodox Jews. We frequently experience limits. However, from the early days of

Christianity, the Christian population in Israel has mixed the theologies of Christianity and Judaism. The strong Jewish culture of modern day Israel tends to even confuse the Israelis concerning the difference between being an Israeli citizen and a practicing Jew. For example, a Christian pastor might teach that belief in the work of Jesus allows them to be adopted as children of Abraham, by faith. However, Jews are already consider themselves children of their father Abraham, ethnically. As adopted Jews by nationality, they are expected to celebrate the feasts and observe the dietary laws. Israelis faith is more than a set of beliefs; it has been a way of life involving economics, social and political attitudes and activities. Faith is the highest value. It has allowed them to survive persecutions and wars for thousands of years.

Bill asked Al, "What caused all this growth, from 12 to 20,000, since 1948?"

"Excellent question," said Al. "It really started early on with an influx of Christian missionaries from the USA during the 1950s. You will see that our brochure quotes Rabbi Lifshitz in the Jerusalem Post of March of 2008, stating, '... Christian missionaries have succeeded in converting around 15,000 Jews to Christianity in

Israel.' Our brochure also points out that the Messianic community sees itself as a legitimate branch of Judaism," and goes on to say; 'The Messianic community believes there is no contradiction between being Jewish and believing Jesus to have been the Savior and the Son of God.' Their numbers have been steadily growing, in large part due to proselytizing activities." Jerusalem Post, March, 2008 "How are these congregations supported? Is it strictly by the donations of its congregants?" asked Liz.

"There are many churches, like Howie Kings back in Rhode Island and other groups from the USA and other parts of the world that channel funds into the hands of Messianic Jewish congregations and ministries in Israel. They also assist in providing humanitarian support for the needy," Al responded.

Al concluded with the following point. "If we continue to grow, at this rapid rate, Messianic Judaism, has the potential to greatly influence the nation of Israel religiously, politically and culturally as well. It's kind of like completing the circle from Jesus' day. It's the key reason why I am thrilled to be a part of it."

Liz said, "And Al, from what I have seen from your dealings with the Israeli government, that influence you speak of is already happening."

"Very astute observation, Liz," said Al.

"It is amazing how much religion surrounds this place, and not just what you would think of, like Islam and Judaism, but then groups like the German sect. I wonder how comfortable Liz and I are really going to be here," mused Bill out loud.

"We'll be just fine honey," said Liz, ever the optimist.

"Actually, Liz is quite right," said Al. "For all its religious heritage, with three major faiths claiming it as Holy, Israel is a very secular society today, for the most part. And there is no typical Israeli, so it is a pretty open society in that way, too. In fact, more than half of the population considers itself secular."

"Secular Jews, that is exactly how you and I describe ourselves." Liz said to Bill. "So, I think we will fit in just fine."

"I guess if we just don't convert to Christianity, we'll fit right in here," Bill commented, looking for a response from the three Christians in the van.

After an awkward pause, Al, the Christian Jew responded.

"Ah, but if you ever did make a commitment to Christ, what more enjoyable place could you find yourselves living, outside of heaven, than in the Holy Land?"

"You are right about that," said Liz.

Elaine and I said "Amen" at the same time. Shortly thereafter we arrived back at the hotel, where Al just dropped us off. Both couples agreed to have dinner separately that night, to catch up on our thoughts and with one another. There were no tensions; it was just time for a break. Besides, the next couple of days we were going to be involved in some intense sightseeing around the Holy City and we knew there would be different emotions for each of us as we encountered them. Elaine and I actually had something sent up to the room, watched a little Israeli TV, and turned in a bit early.

CHAPTER 18

WALKING OLD JERUSALEM

It was one thing to stroll around modern Jerusalem, but now to enter the ancient city of Jerusalem that was something unlike anything we had ever experienced. The reality of it all hit us like a proverbial ton of bricks. We kept looking at each other as we walked the areas that Jesus walked and could not get over the fact that it was all still there, albeit altered somewhat by man and nature over two thousand years. As we saw the various sites, my mind was also flooded with some of the stories I had learned first in Sunday school. It was simply amazing. Liz and Bill also marveled at how well-preserved some things were and that these places were, in fact, real. It was the first time I had ever seen Bill get serious about his Judaism. He remarked more than once how, since this was all real, maybe the stories surrounding it were indeed all real, too. Nothing more divinely insightful than that ever seemed to come forth from him regarding this tour, but that alone was a step of a skeptic in the direction of faith.

The points of interest in Old Jerusalem are all so close to

each other, that tourists get a chance to visit many sites within a short time period. A visitor can get a lot into their itinerary in a hurry. And that is exactly what the ladies and Al had in mind for all of us. The main passage into the Old City is the Jaffa Gate and so that is where we began our tour. We strolled first through the Jewish Quarter, which has been inhabited by Jews as far back as the first Temple, some 3,000 years ago. Today it is a modern neighborhood with several thousand people in it. To get the real flavor of the combination of the old and new of the area, Al took us to the Ha-Kardo, an area the Romans built to hold prisoners after the fall of Jerusalem in A.D. 70

Today it is a quaint market area with modern, trendy shops nearby. Of course, the ladies wanted to visit them all. They had already filled several shopping bags, before Al guided us down to some wide stone steps. Once at the steps, Al told us that an excavation in the 1980s uncovered an outer wall of Jerusalem as it existed during King Hezekiah's reign. He told us that these steps led down to the most important site, not only within the quarter, but perhaps in all of Jewish civilization. He asked us if we could guess what it is.

119

"The Western Wall," smarty pants Elaine fired back, instantly.

"You got it," said Al. "Although it is also referred to as the Wailing Wall."

"This is the wall that is always open and people throng to it continually, both day and night. They are a combination of worshipers and tourists like us," Al explained.

"Why did they call it the Wailing Wall?" Bill asked Al.

"It has to do with the fact that Jews initially flocked here in great numbers to jointly lament over the Romans' destruction of Jerusalem and the Temple about 2,000 years ago. But the wall itself is not really part of the Temple proper," Al went on. "It was merely a retaining wall of the Temple Mount, but it is the only surviving part, so the people naturally gather here."

"Now Liz, take notes," Bill said.

"I am, I am, at least in my head. There is no way that I am going to forget this place," Liz responded. The same could have been said by all of us.

As we observed from the Western Wall, we saw "Harem Esh-Sharif," the Venerable Sanctuary, as the Muslims call it. Then suddenly Liz called out, "Oh my goodness, this is it, this is it, the Temple Mount." And she was right. There, just up from the front of us, was the Temple Mount— the most disputed part of the most tension-filled area of the world, and a key to end-time events. It was also the biggest challenge of Liz's Stein's life.

Liz had been doing her research and had been reading briefs from her government contacts to give her greater insight into her new project. So, she had a whole lot to share with us at this point in our tour. However, we were not allowed to proceed up to the mount because of strict regulations about the time of day we were there.

So we all turned to our guide, Al.

"When we talk about the Temple Mount, what exactly are we talking about?" Bill asked Al.

As Al explained it, "The Temple Mount has been used as a religious site for thousands of years. Four religions have made use of the Temple Mount: Judaism, Christianity, Roman religion, and Islam. It can be ascended via four gates, with guard posts of Israeli police in the vicinity of each. Judaism regards the Temple Mount as the place where God gathered the dust used to create the first man, Adam. It is also the location of Abraham's binding of Isaac. The

121

location is the holiest site in Judaism and is the place Jews turn towards during prayer. It is also widely considered the third holiest site in Islam: as their al-Aqsa Mosque and Dome of the Rock are on the site. The Dome of the Rock currently sits in or close to the area, where Jewish and Christian scholars believe the Bible mandates the Holy Temple be rebuilt. In light of the dual claims of both Judaism and Islam, it is one of the most contested religious sites in the world." Once again, Al had demonstrated his knowledge and skill as a biblical scholar and teacher. As Prime Minister Benjamin Netanyahu explained at one of his frequent briefings; things aren't always tranquil, because of these conflicting beliefs and claims. The evening news ran his remarks, in the context of their reporting, on the same day we visited old Jerusalem. Here is what he had to say,

"JERUSALEM (AP) — Israel's prime minister vowed to maintain longstanding worship arrangements at Jerusalem's most sensitive religious site amid rising tensions in the city.

Palestinian protesters and Israeli police have clashed in east Jerusalem in recent months, with much of the unrest focused on a sacred compound revered by both Jews and Muslims.

It is the holiest site for Jews, who call it the Temple Mount because of the revered Jewish Temples that stood there in biblical times.

Muslims refer to it as the Noble Sanctuary, and it is their third holiest site, after Mecca and Medina in Saudi Arabia.

"Since the days of Abraham, the Temple Mount has been the holiest site for our people and with this, the Temple Mount is also the most sensitive kilometer on earth," Benjamin Netanyahu said.

"Alongside our determined stance for our rights, we are determined to maintain the status quo for all the religions in order to prevent an eruption," he added.

Israel captured east Jerusalem — with its sites sacred to Jews, Muslims and Christians — from Jordan in the 1967 war. Palestinians demand the territory for their future capital. The fate of the area is an emotional issue for Jews and Muslims and its future lies at the heart of the conflict between Israel and the Palestinians.

Muslim worshippers view Jewish prayer at the site as a provocation, and Israeli authorities place tough restrictions on it.

Palestinian President Mahmoud Abbas praised Netanyahu's call for preserving the status quo, calling it a "step in the right direction."

Then Liz changed the discussion's focus somewhat.

"The Islamic influence upon Jerusalem can be seen all around the Old City," Liz said, "and especially in their mosques. In the seventh century Caligh Omar built a mosque on the Temple Mount, and in the eight century it was expanded into what we now see, The Dome of The Rock. Look how beautiful the outside structure of the Dome is, with its outer decoration of mosaics, marble, stained glass and painted tiles. The dome is gold plated aluminum. It truly is an amazing sight and I don't know how the Israeli government expects us to deal with it. I think we must see a way clear to a nearby location that would still be considered part of the greater Temple site," Liz went on explaining and thinking out loud at the same time.

Since, as non-Muslims, we could not venture inside this daunting edifice at this time and definitely not to pray, we had to rely on Al our teacher/guide.

"Once inside, the one thing that stands out is a huge boulder, located underground. A boulder that is sacred to both Jew and Muslim. To the Muslim it is believed to be the spot from which Mohamed ascended into heaven. To the Jews, it reportedly is the rock on which Abraham was going to sacrifice his son Isaac," said Al.

"Boy, this brings it right home doesn't it?" said Elaine.

"What do you mean?" I asked.

"The complexity of the situation," Elaine responded. Both Abraham and Mohammed are about as big as you can get in their respective religions. This rock has such great significance to both faiths that it would cause a holy war if one tried to take it from the other."

"You are absolutely correct," said Al. "Since it is a delicate balance of co-existence, I am afraid that anything too direct or appearing confrontational would easily disrupt that balance, which could lead to an all-out holy war. So, that is precisely why the Israeli government and by extension, Liz, is going to have to work very slowly, wisely and sensitively on the proposed project of a new Temple. However, that doesn't mean it can't be done. And to us Christians, it must be done."

"Yes," Elaine reminded us. "It can and will be done in God's time and in his way, because we already know it is his will."

"And we know, with God all things are possible," I added.

That ended our tour for the day, although Liz went back for a more in depth look at the dome area the next two days with Bill. Only, now she was going to be shadowed by two plain-clothes Israeli security officers.

"They said we should call them Jake and Elroy, like the Blues brothers," Liz said. We all chuckled over that one. Al said the Israeli government insisted on it, due to the sensitive nature of the project that Liz was working on. Liz was enthralled with this area and as she told us later, "This is the beginning of my preparation for the project that my soon-to-be new country is asking me to do for them. I must spend quality time here, learning, observing and getting a feeling for the entire landscape." Bill was just happy to be seeing it all through Liz's eyes. Besides, there was no way he was going to let Liz be there without him, even with security guards.

So Al, Elaine, and I continued on our sightseeing walk through the Old City for the next two days. We walked the Via Dolorosa-the way of the cross, down to the Church of the Holy Sepulcher, which is said to be the site of the death, burial, and resurrection of Christ. We lingered there quite a while, in awe and amazement. On the same day we also visited the Garden Tomb, the Mount of Olives, the Pool of Bethesda, and the Room of the Last Supper. It was a whirlwind tour, but simply inspiring, especially for Elaine and me. Al's running commentary was helpful because he seemed to know everything about all of these places.

On the second day, as Liz and Bill continued their explorations of the dome area, Elaine, Al, and I traveled the short distance down to Bethlehem, which is in Palestinian territory.

Hence, for safety, we travelled by taxi, with a Christian Palestinian driver, who took us directly into Manger Square. We got out at the Church of the Nativity. The church is over the site where tradition says Jesus was born. We entered the church and went downstairs to the Grotto of the Nativity. Al pointed to the floor of the grotto and our eyes quickly turned there and beheld a beautiful gleaming star. Al told us to look at the inscription. It was in Latin, but Al quickly translated it for us. It said, "Here Jesus Christ was born of the Virgin Mary." What a powerful message! Then the three of us went upstairs to the church sanctuary to pray and read Scripture together. I have read Luke chapter two, the Christmas story, to my kids every Christmas day morning, but it never was so vividly alive to me as when we read it in church that day. After we finished and were heading back in the taxi, I said to Al, "Al, you should just become a tour guide. You would be great at it."

"Funny that you should mention that," Al responded. "I have been thinking the very same thing. It's is a true joy for me to visit these wonderful and important places. Then, to share them with others is a joy beyond measure." So maybe we found a new calling for Al.

127

CHAPTER 19

TWO EMPTY TOMBS

We all continued to enjoy the sights of Jerusalem, both old and new, for the remainder of our trip. However, Liz divided her time between being with us and working on her upcoming project. She focused primarily on exploring the Dome of the Rock area. Sometimes Bill and Al went with her and sometimes she was also part of the team of engineers she would be leading, when she moved here. We also spent a long day with Al's Christian realtor friend, Pam Johnson Rosenbaum, who had moved here years earlier from Providence, R.I. Pam tried to locate a place for the Steins to live when they moved to Israel. Liz and Pam hit it off right away. And several places seemed acceptable, so there should be no problem on that front. Bill also kept an eye out for a location for his dreamed of cafe. However, while several areas appeared to be possibilities for a café; that decision could wait until after they moved here.

To Elaine and me, by far the most spiritually moving sight of all we had visited in Israel was the viewing of the empty tomb, both at the Church of the Holy Sepulcher and the Garden Tomb.

Why visit two locations of the one tomb? The tomb location is actually somewhat in dispute. The most accepted location for conservative scholars is the Garden Tomb, because it fits best with the Biblical story of a garden. It is an actual garden setting today and in general proximity to the hill upon which Jesus died on the cross. The local Anglican Church actually oversees this site and host's visitors. It is the site Elaine and I enjoyed the most. We also agreed that it is the site that is most probably the correct location of the tomb.

The location accepted by most Catholics and Orthodox Church members is the one in the Church of the Holy Sepulcher, at the end of the Via Dolorosa. In a way, knowing that there were disputed sites, just reinforced the important thing for us. Namely, the facts that Jesus was resurrected from the dead, was seen by many and then ascended into heaven, from where he will come to earth again. It is not the actual location of his empty tomb. Al, the Bible scholar and outstanding tour guide, spent a good deal of time explaining all about it to us. Elaine and I were in awe as we contemplated the significance of this empty tomb at both locations. That was the most significant fact about it-it was empty! All I could think of was the old Easter song, "He Is Risen, He Is Risen Indeed!" Al stressed the point that if Christ is not risen then Christians are all fools, because we are following a mere mortal and thus we are all still dead in our sins.

At some point Bill said, "It sounds like all of Christianity hinges on that one claim that Jesus rose from the dead."

"Exactly right." said Al.

"Then why doesn't somebody just disprove the resurrection and all of Christianity can go away and only two religious, Judaism and Islam can lay religious claim to the Holy Land?" asked Liz.

"Haven't many tried to do just that?" asked Elaine.

"They sure have," said Al. "The only trouble is they couldn't do it because the evidence did not support their contention. The clear evidence supports the amazing claim that Jesus did come out of the tomb and was seen by many, before he ascended into heaven."

"I especially like the story of one man who tried to disprove the resurrection. Frank Morison, a British journalist who set out to examine the evidence first-hand, as he would in a courtroom case, thinking, he would disprove Christianity once and for all, by controverting the evidence of its foundational claim, the resurrection of Jesus Christ from the dead. Although, that was his pen name. His real name was Albert Henry Ross.

"What is it with these writers and their pen-names? I mean first we learned about George Orwell really being Eric Blair and now this guy. Doesn't anybody use their own name to write a book anymore?" Bill interrupted.

"I don't know, but I have a friend named Ray, who writes under the pen-name Frank, so apparently it is still common," I responded.

"In any event, if he had succeeded, we would not be here today as Christians viewing any tombs, and our Christianity would be reduced to just a set of moral teachings from a man who lived 2,000 years ago," Al explained.

"What was the result of his quest?" asked Bill.

"He did study the evidence and he did write a book about it, originally published in the early 30's. It is entitled, '*Who Moved The Stone?'* In the book, he does present the evidence, as it would have been in a court room. He also expressed his conclusion clearly, by stating, 'This is surely evidence that demands a verdict!' "Al explained.

"What was his verdict?" asked Liz.

"I will wait to answer that one, because I think it would make for a great discussion over dinner tonight, and I know this great little café," Al coyly.

"You are such a tease, Al Hoffman!" Elaine said.

"He is, but given the fact that Al is a believer, provides a major clue as to what the 'verdict' will be." I suggested.

"Safe bet. I will even take the odds on that one," said Bill.

We all laughed. The idea of extending the discussion over tonight's dinner seemed reasonable and not too long a wait. Al had certainly whet our appetites, and not just for food.

CHAPTER 20

EVIDENCE AND VERDICT

Al took us to Café Focaccia, where the food was excellent, as with our previous dining experiences since arriving. And the ambiance — well, let's just say it was very old-world Middle Eastern. For example, the interior is small and mostly made of stone; and the food includes sheep cheese; sabich pita, an eggplant dish, shawarma, a grilled lamb, or sometimes turkey dish and a tasty black olive spread. We actually all had pasta dishes and they were outstandingly delicious.

"Okay, so what was the verdict of the author in *Who Moved the Stone?*" Bill started in on Al during appetizers. "Did I win my bet? He changed his mind, didn't he?"

"Bingo," Al shot back. "You win the prize. Frank Morison, having set out to disprove the resurrection and thereby destroy Christianity once and for all, concluded that the evidence pointed to the fact that Jesus rose from the dead; so his verdict was that the claims of the resurrection were true."

"Wow, that was quite a turnaround," Elaine remarked.

"I'll say!" exclaimed Liz.

"Okay I'll bite," Bill offered. "What changed his mind?"

"I don't exactly know, but it seems to have begun when he started to look at the other options," Al responded.

"What other options?" asked Bill.

"Let's think about it. What other options could there possibly be for an empty tomb?" queried Al.

"The disciples stole the body back," suggested Liz.

"That's one," said Al.

"His enemies, the religious leaders who had him crucified, stole the body," contributed Elaine.

"That certainly is another option," said Al.

"There are more options?" asked Bill.

Keeping the conversation going; I asked, "What if he really never died?" Then continuing, I pressed the issue. "You know, maybe he wasn't dead when they took him down from the cross. Later he revived in the tomb, came out, and just disappeared."

Al, the scholars quickly responded, "There is a name for that theory. It is called the Swoon Theory. Now, if you think it through, there is only one other option. Can anyone come up with it?"

"I don't know, but in my view, they were all hallucinating when they claimed to see him out of his grave. At least that would be my guess," Bill opined.

"The hallucination theory; you are exactly right Bill," Al quickly responded.

"Doctor, you are such a brainiac," I joked.

Al, picking up on Bill's point, then continued, "Since you brought it up Bill, let's start by examining the hallucination argument."

"First we have the utterance of Mary of Magdala, who said, 'I have seen him with my own eyes,' " Al stated.

"Yes, but she could have imagined it," Bill theorized.

"You're right. She may have had a hallucination during her period of grief," Al agreed.

"Yes, it could have been all in her head," Bill responded.

"But wasn't he also seen by others?" Elaine asked.

"You're correct again. He also was seen by Peter that same day, and by the entire group of disciples that night, minus one. Only the disciple Thomas was not there. Later, when he was told they had seen Jesus, Thomas did not believe it, so he is often called, Doubting

Thomas." Al explained.

"Well, as a doctor, I know that hallucinations do happen and people are sometimes deluded," Bill added.

"Of course, but would you also agree that hallucinations are highly individualized, subjective experiences, and that it is extremely rare for even two people to have the same hallucination?" Al asked Bill.

"Perhaps, but maybe this was a one-in-a-million hallucination, because all the disciples wanted to believe it so badly," Bill again theorized.

"But they didn't want to believe it," I blurted out.

"They didn't want to believe it, what do you mean? I thought they were waiting to see him arise from the dead on the third day, as he promised to do?" Liz entered into the discussion.

"From the biblical account, the disciples were a pretty discouraged group after the crucifixion. They were not at all predisposed to believing Jesus was alive again and of course the worst was Doubting Thomas, who said he wouldn't believe unless he felt the nail-pierced hands," Al responded quickly.

"Where and when were the other appearances?" asked Liz.

"Off the top of my head and not necessarily in order, Jesus appeared to Mary of Magdala, to Peter, and to two followers of his who did not even recognize him, while they walked together on the road to the town of Emmaus. The walk from Jerusalem to Emmaus is about seven miles, so they walked and talked together for a long period of time. No delusions or hallucinations apparent there. Moving on, he was also seen by his human brother, James, by some women returning from the tomb, and later to a group of around 500 of his followers. That would be a massive, and dare I say unbelievable hallucination. On another occasion he saw seven of his disciples by the Sea of Tiberias and had breakfast with them. And, most famously, he appeared to Doubting Thomas. Thomas proclaimed at that time and after a cursory examination of the wounds to Jesus' hands and side, 'my Lord and my God!'" rejoined Al.

"Wow, you are quite the Bible scholar! And, skeptic that I am, I have to confess that the so-called hallucination theory would be quite a stretch to argue, as an explanation of what happened. It would take more faith to believe that than to believe in the fact that a man came back from the dead," said Bill.

"I agree with my husband totally on this point. Logically, there is no rational way to explain away Jesus meetings at so many places with so many people as hallucinations. Either you believe the biblical account or you do not. So, why don't we just move on to the next possible explanation," said Liz.

"Very well put, said Al. Then let's continue, and remember, there are only a very few options as to what happened to Jesus."

"Well, exactly what are the other options?" asked Elaine.

"Besides the hallucination theory, you have the swoon theory, which posits that Jesus never really died on the cross, but was revived later in the tomb; the disciples stole the body is a third explanation; or his enemies stole the body; and lastly, Jesus is alive because God raised him from the dead on the third day," said Al.

"The hallucination theory is already out number one, so let's get batter number two up," I urged excitedly.

"I already can see problems with his enemies stealing the body," said Liz." When the disciples started going around preaching that he was raised from the dead, all his enemies would have had to do to disprove it, would be to parade the dead body around Jerusalem."

"You are spot on," said Al. "Why would his enemies steal the body if it were not for the purpose of presenting it at the right moment publicly? They hated Christ and they could have nipped this new religious movement in the bud, so to speak, by exposing it and embarrassing their enemies."

"Okay, maybe, but what about the possibility that the disciples stole the body? Didn't they have a lot to gain by keeping up a hoax like this one? Fame, influence, money, power?" asked Bill.

To answer, Al went on to explain that the stolen body theory creates more questions than it answers, especially if the body had been taken by the disciples.

"For example?" I asked.

"Let's walk through it," said Al.

Al further developed his case by raising a few key questions.

"If the guards were sleeping how could they have known if the body was stolen, and by whom? The penalty for a Roman soldier sleeping on guard duty was execution. So, would all the Roman guards have decided to take a nap at the same time? Even if the soldiers were sleeping, how would the disciples have known about it? Joseph was given the body and he put it in the tomb and rolled the stone in place. He and perhaps Nicodemus, could have been hiding in the bushes and waited until all the guards were asleep, then stole the body. However, even if they did, how did they manage to roll the stone along a grooved incline without the soldiers hearing them? And, if they accomplished that Herculean feat, how did they then subsequently steal the body without awakening even one of the Roman guards?"

"Let's say they did find a way to do it, then that could explain it all, if the disciples had the body, right?" Bill asked.

"Bill, surely you must admit that it is harder to believe that one, than the actual miracle of the resurrection?" I challenged him.

"Maybe or maybe not: perhaps they found a way," Bill responded.

"Okay, let's say for a moment that it happened, that the disciples stole the body; now we have other questions challenging us," said Al.

"Like what?" asked Liz.

"No, actually like why?" Al responded.

"Why what?" asked Bill.

"Why would the disciples want to steal the body of their fallen leader?" Al quickly responded.

"I don't know and I am getting a bit confused with all of this information overload, especially with everything else going on right now in my head," Liz responded.

"And we need to let your escorts get some rest, too," said Bill.

"What are you talking about?" Liz asked.

"Aren't the guys sitting at the bar Jake and Elroy, your guards from the other day?" Bill responded.

"Oh, you know, you're right. I hadn't even noticed them. They just probably come here when they're off duty," said Liz.

"Liz is probably right," said Al. "However, I know that the government is concerned about word of this project eventually leaking out and causing some unrest among our enemies. So, if they are here to keep an eye on you, it is just a measure of precaution."

"That really bothers me," said Bill "Maybe this assignment is really something more dangerous than we ever anticipated. Especially, since you are an American. We're not the most popular people in this area of the world."

"Oh, come on honey," Liz responded. "Like Al said, it is strictly precautionary and it could be just a coincidence that they are here at all."

"No, you are probably right," said Bill.

"Why can't we end the speculation and just ask them?" I asked

With that simple, yet logical question, we all agreed to end the speculation.

Bill and Al approached them and then returned to us shortly thereafter. We were right; they have been assigned to Liz for the entire remainder of her visit, as a precautionary measure. Apparently, the area we visited the other day when we were looking at the Temple area is known for its radical Palestinian sympathizers. So, we probably should not have had lunch in the café where we did. However, the Israeli engineers we were with didn't know and they picked the place.

"And Jake and Elroy Blues over there didn't want to interfere, so they just sat at the bar and watched out for you," Bill explained.

"Jake and Elroy," I said. "What's with those names?"

"That is how they want us to refer to them. It is just part of their standard operating procedure not to use real names. The less we know, the less we could reveal under duress. It also helps all of us not to get too personal with them. The tall one is Elroy and the shorter one is Jake," Explained Al.

"They also said to not worry. They would not bother us and just to enjoy the rest of our time in Israel," Bill added. "So, I suggest that is exactly what we do."

We all agreed with Bill and also agreed to leave the resurrection topic there, for now. It was time to let our brains rest and enjoy our meal and so that is what we did. Al informed us that he wanted to take us for an overnight sightseeing trip tomorrow. We all readily agreed to go. He then told us that he would pick us up after breakfast, to pack an overnight bag and be sure to include our bathing suits. Beyond that, he would not tell us a thing about the trip. Just like Al, trying to have a little fun and build excitement, I thought.

CHAPTER 21

DOWN TO THE SEA IN A VAN

After breakfast the very next morning Al came by with his van as planned, and we all piled into it. He said we were going on a trip to visit an Old Salt and the Alamo of the Jews. As we rode east down Route 1, we all tried to guess what in the world he was talking about. This guessing game lasted practically the whole ride. I am sure that is what Al was hoping for on this trip. He would not even give us a hint whenever we did venture a guess. He just kept driving, played music and pointed out some sites as we passed them. Finally, we started to get some clues as the signs appeared for "Route 90 S, via The Dead Sea." Sure enough, Al turned off Route one, onto Route 90 S. We all shouted it about the same instant: "The Old Salt is The Dead Sea!" Al just laughed and said, "Took you long enough. We've only been riding for about an hour and forty-five minutes."

Awhile later, we turned off onto Route 31. The road was all downhill to the seashore. "Hold on to your hats. This is going to get a bit dramatic," said Al.

We did not know exactly what he meant. However, it soon

became apparent. From that point, the ride down to The Dead Sea was only about fifteen miles, but it seemed like forever on a downhill roller coaster ride. It snaked through canyons, cliffs, and tiny valleys the entire way. We kept urging Al to pay attention to the road. Once we arrived at the Dead Sea, Al made a pronouncement. "Ladies and gentlemen, you are now at 1,292 feet below sea level. Hence, when you step out onto the shore in a moment, you will all be literally at the lowest point on planet earth."

He told us that the Dead Sea, once the summer beach area to King Herod and the source of Cleopatra's cosmetic raw materials, is known today for cleansing and moisturizing. Many claim that it has additional therapeutic benefits as well. We could hardly wait to swim in it. However, first we had to drive down the road a bit to our hotel, where Al had already made reservations for us. We confirmed them and then went up to our rooms to freshen up. A short while later, we were back at the seashore. We floated about on the dense sea, and played some, too. You can only imagine the fun we had taking the black mud and putting it all over each other. The black mud is enriched soil that not only is therapeutic, but also supposedly has beauty-enhancement properties. However, all I really know is

145

that it made for a lot of fun in the sun for the Steins and the Morettis that day. We returned to our hotel in the late afternoon and then met in the hotel restaurant for dinner around seven. We talked mostly about the day and all the fun at the beach. Al finally shared that the day of fun was not over because he also had booked us for spa treatments, followed by a dip in a warm sulfur pool. Al said he was also picking up the tab for it, but he was going to bed right after dinner and a brief stroll. No, you can't find a better tour guide than Al, I thought, or a better friend.

Before leaving the table, Al said, "Let's meet for breakfast around ten, packed and ready for, 'the Alamo of Israel,' okay?"

"You got it Al," said Bill.

With that, it was off to the spa and sulfur pool. What a great day in all our lives!

We ate a hearty breakfast that next morning at the hotel. We thanked Al for the spa and sulfur pool fun and shared about the wonderful day we had experienced. Then we started to quiz Al about our upcoming visit to what he told us was the "Alamo of Israel," and tried to guess at that one. However, typical of Al, he would not let on if we were right or even hot or cold. So, we just decided to wait and see. He did tell us to put on our hiking boots for this one. Before breakfast concluded, Al pulled an Elaine tactic on us. He gave us all a notebook* about the empty tomb, filled with verses and arguments we had already gone over about what might have happened to the body of Jesus, if the resurrection were not true. He also put some quotes in there by Frank Morison the author of *Who Moved the Stone?*

I'm sure you'll recall that Frank was the skeptic journalist turned believer that Al had spoken to us about in our previous discussions.

"Just keep in mind, Al said to us, "This guy wrote over a century ago, so his English is old style and sometimes a bit hard to follow."

"Kind of like the King James version of the Bible?" Elaine asked.

"Well, it wasn't written that far back, but there are some similarities," Al responded.

We accepted Al's notebook without any real discussion. I don't think anyone wanted another heavy debate that particular morning. However, we all promised to look over and ruminate on

Al's notebook, thoroughly. Then we finished packing, checked out,

jumped into Al's van and headed for "The Alamo!"

*Appendices B, Al's Resurrection Evidence Notebook

CHAPTER 22

AL'S ALAMO

Al's "Alamo," as it turned out, was actually the ancient Jewish mountaintop fortress called Masada. A flat topped mountain, Masada is undergirded by steep, rigid and rocky cliffs on all sides. Today, it offered us spectacular views of both the Dead Sea and the desert. The natural plateau surrounding Masada makes it a nearly impregnable fortress. It was built by King Herod the Great. Brilliant at construction engineering for his day, he developed Masada in the first century on about eighteen acres. All of us, but especially Liz were very impressed with this image of the King of the Jews during the time of Christ. The image of Herod, as King of the Jews was the main reason he was so jealous and outraged when Jesus began to be referred to by that same title, King of the Jews. Masada was built for both protection and recreation. For example, it had several palaces, storehouses, and a sophisticated water system, a surrounding wall, and garrisons for Herod's troops.

"I think that because you are Jewish, you can have confidence for your role in the rebuilding of the Temple. Your

Jewish ancestors certainly demonstrated at Masada, that you come from a great heritage of building genius," Elaine said to Liz. "You sure do," I commented. "Oh you guys are so encouraging and kind. But this is making me wonder what I have gotten myself into," said Liz. "You must admit that our ancestors were certainly brilliant in the area of building, so it must be in your genes someplace," Bill responded. "They certainly were," Al commented, "but they were up against the Romans, who were the best in the world at that time." "Thanks for pointing that out," I said. "I figured you would appreciate my pointing that out," said Al, teasing. Then Al said, "The Romans let Herod serve as King of the Jews, while they really reigned over the land. However, after the Jews began to rebel against Rome in AD 66 Rome destroyed Jerusalem in AD 70, causing many rebels to flee to Masada. Thus Masada became the last Jewish stronghold until it was finally over run in AD 73 by the Roman armies. In the meantime, men, women, and their children lived at Masada and were protected by its cliffs of over 1,400 feet high."

"What happened? How did the Romans get up these cliffs to attack?" asked Liz.

Al responded, "After almost a year, the Roman legions

finally completed an assault ramp, giving them access to the mountaintop on Masada's western side. After hearing a rousing speech by their leader, Elazar Ben-Yair, on the evening before the Romans attacked, the remaining rebels decided to kill themselves rather than surrender to the Romans. At least, that is the inspirational story passed down from some of the family survivors.

The story was told to and recorded by the famous Roman historian, Flavius Josephus. When the Romans finally breached the wall the next morning, they found hundreds of corpses. Thus ended the last stand of the Jews against Rome. Because it reminds me of the Texans' last stand against the huge Mexican army, I think of it as the Jewish Alamo. So, I guess you could say that Elazar Ben-Yair is to the Jews, what Davey Crockett is to Americans."

At least that is what Al believed, and who are we to disagree with Al?

To tour Masada, we took a ride up on a cable car and then walked the path known as Snake Path, to get to the top. Once there, we were able to view Herod's palaces and other structures, along with spectacular views of the desert so far below. Al, ever our tour guide, made sure that we were informed about all aspects of the fortress, and there were a number of them. Here is just a sampling of what Al introduced us to on that day. He explained to us that the Romans established eight base camps surrounding the mountain, to prevent any escapes, or so no one could come down on them in a surprise attack. They are also the oldest, best kept examples of Rome's armies preparing for battle, left in the entire world.

On the northern precipice, are the ruins of Herod's palace, which boasted Greek themed architecture and Herod's personal bathhouse, which featured amenities such as both cold and mildly warm baths, frescos, tile work, a sauna, and a spa.

Liz paid close attention to all this and started to take notes.

Another interesting item from this Jewish settlement was the Mikveh. Al pointed out that according to Jewish religious tradition, a Mikveh was a ritual bath. He also said it was symbolic of life and hope for all Jews who bathed in it.

Bill said, that he was so impressed with the Mikvehs that he thought Liz should include them in the new Temple and that he also wanted one in their home. Liz, appearing awestruck at this point, just gave a perplexed look back to him. We finally left Masada in the late afternoon and drove nearly three hours back to our hotel in

Jerusalem. Yes, we stopped for a bite to eat along the way. We were exhausted but thrilled to have experienced Masada.

CHAPTER 23

RETURN TO TEL AVIV

The following morning we packed up everything and headed up to Tel Aviv. Liz had one more set of meetings with Israeli officials and her engineering team the next day. The meetings were scheduled to last until about 3 pm. They also included some security briefings from high-level government officials. Al was also invited to these briefings, since he was Liz's official liaison from the Israeli government. We found out later that these briefings were part of a regular series of security updates for government workers. After the presentation sessions, they were edited for sensitive information and subsequently shown on Israeli TV. Hence, Al and Liz were free to share a good deal of what they learned at the briefings with us. Al told us that Israel's government is so continually threatened from all sides, that it wants its people to be fully aware and fully prepared at all times. This is really a unique approach when compared to America and the rest of Israeli's allies. Since our plane was not scheduled to leave until 10 pm, we planned to enjoy our last meal together at the hotel tomorrow night.

However, this was going to be our last night the four friends were going to be together in Israel and we were determined to make a great time of it. The evening was strictly filled with dinner, dancing, strolling and a bit of romancing. It was just the four of us.

"When do we sleep? On the plane!" That was the common refrain for most all-night party people in Tel Aviv, or so we were told. Our favorite eating place of the night was Pops and Martha Booth's Café. Unusual name, but it is one of the most popular night spots in Tel Aviv, especially for the more mature set like the four of us. We loved its food, and really appreciated its mellow and friendly vibe. We mostly ate appetizers of all varieties, wanting to catch as much of the food specialties as we could on this last night. For example, we had potato croquettes, skewered sirloin, and a variety of finger foods.

"My mother used to make potato croquettes and these taste just like hers," I said. "They sure do," Billy agreed.

"Maybe they somehow got a hold of Momma Viola's recipe," Elaine commented.

We all had to nod our heads in agreement and laugh.

We left Pops and Martha Booth's Café around 9 pm and

made our way down to Lilenbaum and Allenby Streets in the Florentine section, because this is where most of the night life is located. We decided to go there later in the evening because things don't really start rocking until 10 pm or so. We arrived at Chelsea's Gold Medal Club a little after 10 pm and it was very crowded. That didn't stop the four of us, as we got out on the dance floor and did our best to look hip, dancing with our improvised gyrations to the latest music. And the music was spun by two gorgeous and talented twin sisters. DJ's, Jessi and Cassy, spun non-stop, among a raucous crowd, until around 3 am. So we kept on dancing, with a few breaks in between, until that time. No, it wasn't exactly as if we were back at the Senior Prom. However, there we were, still dancing the night away, as we had so long ago.

During our walk, we expressed some similar thoughts to one another. Such as how we especially loved the fact that the music tended to be more from our era, the 1970s. And some of these songs did remind us of our prom night and that was fun. So, like so many tourists, we had gone down to the Florentine section and stayed up late, soaking in our final fun night in Israel. And, why not? We were facing a long flight home tomorrow night and would probably do much of that napping. We walked back to our hotel, like four teenagers in love. What a great trip it had been.

CHAPTER 24

A MAJOR CRISIS

Getaway day was upon us and we were all packed and ready for it. The five of us were now enjoying our last delicious meal together at one of the hotel restaurants.

We casually reviewed our great trip and then the discussion turned to the briefings that Liz and Al attended.

"So, what can you tell us," Elaine asked?

"Fill us in," quipped Bill.

With that, both Al and Liz started to zero in on the concerns of Israel regarding their unfriendly neighbors and their surrogate groups, such as Hamas, Hezbollah and now Isis, among a number of others.

Al brought along an edited briefing notebook and began to quote to us from it.

It proved to be informative and unnerving at the same time.

Al started, "The representative of Palestine Media quoted this translation of a piece from a leader of the Muslim Brotherhood. It speaks to their global agenda and refers to Hassan al-Banna the founder of the Muslim Brotherhood who said the following:

He (al-Banna) felt ... the urgent need and obligation which Islam places on every Muslim...to act in order to restore the Islamic Caliphate ...the banner of Jihad has already been raised...and it will continue to be raised...until every inch of Islam ...will be established."

Al explained, "Here is what several speakers said of the so-called Arab Spring of 2011, when more radical governments were formed following takeovers in Egypt, Libya, and Yemen. They minced no words."

So here's the bottom line. There's a new power in the Middle East. It is an alliance of the Muslim Brotherhood groups already ruling the Gaza Strip (Hamas), Egypt and Tunisia, Libya, Syria and Jordan. ...They are all dedicated to revolution...and genocide against the Jews...

The group, Human Rights Watch, reported the following information to us," said Liz. "In late August 42 Christian churches across Egypt had been attacked. The recent attacks have been unusually violent and widespread. Christians reported that security forces did little or nothing to stop the attacks. Observers said the Muslim Brotherhood was behind the attacks.

One Christian leader, unnamed, wrote, "Please continue to pray for my country. Peaceful Egypt is now soaked into violence, hatred and desire to revenge. My heart and the hearts of millions of Christian and Muslim Egyptians are bleeding as we see Egypt turn into a strange country we've never known before.

Ever since Islamists took office...they have been trying to convince us that they are advocates of moderation, democracy, women's rights and individual freedom. ...now we can see that these Islamic

159

groups are taking us for fools.

Liz and Al also heard from Israeli Prime Minister Benjamin Netanyahu at the briefing.

"The Prime Minister reiterated the remarks that he had already given to the US Congress in 2011 on the so called Arab Spring, which some now refer to as the Islamist Winter," explained Liz.

The extraordinary scenes in Tunis and Cairo evoke those of Berlin and Prague in 1989. Yet as we share their hopes, we must also remember that those hopes could be snuffed out as they were in Tehran in 1979. You remember what happened then. The brief democratic spring in Iran was cut short by a ferocious and unforgiving tyranny…so today, the Middle East stands at a fateful crossroads. Like all of you, I pray that the people of the region choose the path less travelled, the path of liberty.

"He also spoke of Iran's nuclear threat at another point," said Al.

Is there such a thing as a suicidal regime? You can't rule it out. …the greatest challenge …to world peace is the marriage of a militant Islamic regime with nuclear weapons. The…danger is called Iran.

"When Deputy Prime Minister Moshe Ya'alon spoke, he warned us about Iran's nuclear capability in these words," said Liz.

…Iran is developing a missile with a six-thousand mile range.

Missile expert Uzi Rubin later added,

…Iran now has about four hundred Shahab Ballistic Missiles…You only need one (with a nuclear warhead).

Liz and Al agreed that all of this points to a global and not just a regional agenda for Iran.

However, to us, the most alarming part of the briefing was what Al and Liz told us about the possibilities of a renewed Holy War over Jerusalem that could be just around the corner, so to speak. Angele and Miriam, two Mossad agents, gave this part of the briefing. They both expressed fear that the decades-old conflict was moving beyond the traditional nationalist struggle between two peoples fighting for their homelands and spiraling into far-reaching religious confrontation between Jews and Muslims.

Angele said that Jerusalem has recently been a center of clashes, protests and deadly attacks that began over one of the city's major flash points, the Temple Mount, which also harbors the al-Aqsa mosque, the third-most holy-site in Islam.

Miriam also pointed out that at the Vatican, Pope Francis condemned the synagogue killings and urged both sides to " put an end to the spiral of hatred and violence and make courageous decisions for reconciliation and peace."

However, according to Liz and Al, Israel appeared to be moving toward more aggressive actions, which seemed likely to provoke Palestinian outrage and possible backlash. For example, they pointed out that Israel's public security minister, Yitzhak Achubirco, announced that he would "ease restrictions" on Israelis carrying guns for self-defense. And Economy Minister Naftali Manoj called on the government to launch a military operation to "go to the source" of terror in the holy city.

"That is kind of unsettling," said Elaine.

"Yeah, but that stuff happens from time to time. What I want to know is, there anything on ISIL?" Bill asked pointedly.

According to Dawn C., the presenter from an Assyrian freelance newspaper, "ISIS, or the Islamic State, as they now like to refer to themselves, has emptied Mosul, Iraq of most Christians. Mosul is Iraq's second largest city. Their method was simple; they dispersed leaflets that warned, 'Convert, pay jisya, (a tax on non-Muslims), leave – or die.' They have also persecuted Muslims by killing numerous Suni and their Mullah religious leaders. In so doing they were making a statement — they would not tolerate any

162

other interpretation of the Quran, but their own distorted version," Al responded.

On a somewhat more positive note, Liz said, that one briefing presenter, Nora M. from Business News in Tunisia, pointed out that "After years of stormy discussions and intellectual tug-of-war, Tunisia has emerged as a secular democracy. It has adopted a new constitution. It recognizes Islam as its official religion, but affirms the rule of law as secular, thereby allowing for equal treatment for women and minorities."

"Now, if other countries in the region would follow that example, there is a chance of some hope for the future. At least in the near term," said Liz.

We were continuing to discuss the briefing data and finishing supper when Liz asked, "Our waiter sure looks familiar; has anyone else noticed that, too?"

"You know, now that you mention it Honey, I think you're right," agreed Bill.

"I got it," said Liz. "He's the same waiter that we had at the small café, the day we went to lunch with the government engineers, following our visit to the Old Temple area."

Bill waved the waiter over and asked him if he were also a waiter at another place. He told us that he works two jobs and that his other job was at the café the group had lunched at days earlier. Then before he walked away to continue his duties, he said, "My name is Boaron Belimaodavncinsmity (or at least that is how it sounded phonetically) and I hope you will remember me."

Beyond that, it seemed that he was too busy for casual conversation this morning, although they remembered him as being very engaging and talkative while he waited on them at the café. That day he had asked them if they were Americans, and also had told them that he had noticed the whole group walking about and taking pictures of rocks and ruins, across from the café. He had commented that tourists don't usually take pictures there, so we must be planning to build something. Bill had let it slip out to the waiter that he had guessed that right. He also bragged that his wife was going to help build something big and the tourists would gather to take pictures of it for many years to come.

"Small world," quipped Bill.

"Small Jerusalem," Al rejoined.

Just then a women approached our table.

She stated, "I am Lelin Tucboxsata, (or again, at least that is how it sounded phonetically) from the concierge desk." Then she said that she had been asked by a gentleman named Elroy to convey a message to Liz that the black SUV was being brought from the parking garage to the front hotel doors in few minutes. Apparently Jake and Elroy were going to take Liz to her final meeting with the Israeli officials, regarding her Temple work. Liz told the concierge messenger to please let Elroy know that she would be out in less than five minutes. Then, just like the waiter, the concierge lady said, "Again, my name is Lelin Tucboxsata, and I hope that you will remember it."

I remember thinking that it was odd that both should ask us to remember their names, but maybe it was just a local customary thing to say. Perhaps that is also what others in our group were thinking, but no one commented.

Liz was all set for the meeting and had already packed her luggage for our return flight home, which was scheduled for later that day. Bill and I had helped Al put all our items in his van, so we were just going to relax around the hotel until Liz returned. As great as this trip had been, we were all tired and looking forward to returning to the good old USA.

Liz kissed Bill, said "see you later" to all of us at the table, then she got up to leave the restaurant and head towards the front of the hotel. Al got up to accompany her, so there would be no problem communicating with Jake and Elroy. We then turned our attention back to our breakfast conversation, when all of a sudden shots rang out and we could hear screaming and yelling coming from just outside the hotel. We all raced to see what was happening. By the time we got there, we got a glimpse of Liz being pushed into the SUV by the concierge lady, while a guy in the back seat, was trying to blindfold and gag Liz. Elroy had been shot up pretty badly. We soon learned that our waiter had shot him from behind as he struggled with the concierge, who was trying to push Liz in the vehicle, along with two guys who had apparently been waiting nearby for the SUV. They had started the shooting as they were also trying to push Liz into the vehicle. Al, who was now way ahead of us, lunged to grab Liz. Dear Al was shot up pretty badly for his very heroic efforts. Elroy, still barely alive, yelled to Elaine to call 555-5555 on his phone for Mossad, the Israeli version of the CIA. He said to tell them that the three men and one woman who took Liz, sounded like Palestinians. The police were already starting to arrive, apparently called by some bystanders. Jake, who was also shot, but less badly than Elroy, immediately commandeered a taxi. Bill and I jumped in right behind him.

Jake yelled at the driver, "Follow that car!" These were words that I had heard only in movies before.

As we sped away, I was yelling to Elaine to stay with Al and PRAY!

Trying to follow the SUV through the narrow, winding, loud and crowded streets of Tel Aviv proved hair-raising, but the taxi driver was skillful and he was into the challenge at this point. Although we could see the black SUV way ahead of us, we knew it would not be long before we lost sight of it, especially since it was heading for the main highway out of town. We were about fifty yards behind the SUV when it started to move onto the highway and we were losing ground – despite the fact that Bill was continually screaming at the driver to go faster. The truth is that the taxi driver already had "the pedal to the metal," as we used to say. However, it didn't much matter, as we were soon forced to a skidding stop by a large food delivery truck when it crossed the intersection just in front of us. The truck did a slow roll through the intersection, its contents of fruits and vegetables falling onto the street. Now, we were all yelling for the truck to get moving faster, but the driver just continued to take his time, before eventually leaving us enough room to slip through the intersection and over the slippery, slimy fruits and vegetables.

By now, the SUV was long gone. We still continued the pursuit onto the highway, but never did find the SUV again. Later, we learned from Jake, who had spoken to the police, that the truck block was part of the kidnappers' plan of escape. He told us that the truck had been stolen and the driver had been killed earlier that morning.

Mossad agents finally caught up with us and brought us back to their headquarters, where we were reunited with Elaine and said goodbye to Jake, who was heading to a hospital to get his wounds cared for, finally. Elaine had already texted Dan at the store, friends and several prayer chains back home. It wouldn't be long before the American media got wind of the unfolding events, too, and Elaine wanted Dan and Hugo and everyone that we were close to back home to hear it from us first, at least to the degree possible.

Naturally, Bill was angry and completely beside himself with anxiety and a frustration tending towards despair. To be perfectly honest, I think Elaine and I were feeling some of those things too, but we were trying to be strong for Bill.

"Joe, what can we do, what can we do?" Bill cried out to me, his eyes filling with tears. "Moving to Israel, what were we thinking?"

"Look what I got us into."

I just hugged him and said that we all needed to be strong for Liz right now. What else could I say? Stunned by what had taken place, none of us had come close to experiencing anything like this before.

CHAPTER 25

CRISIS MANAGEMENT

After nearly an hour, Israeli special agents Nate Kravitz and Mike Able from Shin Bin, the Israeli version of our Secret Service, came into the room where we were gathered and gave us a full appraisal of the situation, which was not very encouraging. According to their sources Liz was probably taken to a secret location in Gaza. Mike was fairly certain that she would be held for some kind of negotiation for prisoners and a ransom. Shin Bin, Mossad, top Israeli government leaders, and American State Department and CIA officials had already been notified and were gathering at Mossad headquarters to discuss the abduction. As Nate was finishing his initial briefing to us, three American officials showed up. James, Tim and Sam introduced themselves and said it would be best to keep things on a first-name basis. They explained that they were from the U.S. State Department and that they were going to move us to the American Embassy where we would be safe. Soon afterwards we were taken to the Embassy under strong security and by a circuitous route. We eventually arrived at the back of the

170

building and went through an underground tunnel before getting on an elevator. The elevator took us to the first floor. From there we proceeded to a large reception room. As soon as we entered the reception room, we were greeted by Ambassador Roger Kaplan and his wife, Deborah. They escorted us to a lovely and very comfortable American- style living room. Roger and Debbie, as they insisted we refer to them, were very gracious, sensitive and hospitable hosts. They both assured us that we would be their guests and their top priority during this awful crises. So as Roger said to us, "Look at it this way, 'mi casa e tu casa,' my house is your house, as my Italian mother might say." And then Debbie added, graciously and thoughtfully, "It belongs to all Americans. We just happen to be the present occupants." Besides, there was no going home under these circumstances. We certainly did not want to leave Bill's side, either, until this nightmare was brought to a conclusion. Ambassador Kaplan was naturally quiet and reserved, yet professional. He was very kind and reassuring to all of us, especially to Bill. He told us that he had already spoken to the President, who assured him that all the resources of the American government would be used to find Liz and bring her home safely, and that the Israelis promised the same

171

support in this joint effort.

"Do you have any more information? Please let us know what you know," Bill pressed the Ambassador.

"This is what I have at present," said the Ambassador. "First of all, here is a copy of the email and news release that our State Department has just put out to the American and international media. Please read it."

Bill quickly grabbed it from the Ambassador's hand and began reading it to us.

"Attention Ambassador Kaplan:

A member loyal to the Islamic State in Palestine, a disavowed off-shoot of Al Qaeda and an organization which has captured swaths of territory in Palestine and elsewhere recently, has claimed responsibility for Liz's kidnapping. You can read the following news release for more details. Undersecretary of State, Michele Cote Cook.

WASHINGTON (AP)

The Islamic State of Palestine, a radical militant group, is holding an American woman hostage who was doing engineering work in Israel, a state department official said today. The 56-year-old

172

woman is the third American known to have been kidnapped by this same militant group during the past year.

The Islamic State of Palestine recently threatened to kill American hostages if the U.S. does not negotiate with them. It is against U.S. policy to negotiate with any group that it deems to be a terrorist organization and not a legitimate government.

The woman, who was working with a group of Israeli engineers, was kidnapped right in front of her hotel in Tel Aviv. U.S. Officials asked that the woman not be identified out of fear for her safety. All spoke on condition of anonymity.

It is believed that the Islamic State of Palestine militant group is seeking to create a caliphate across the Middle East. The militant group is so ruthless in its attacks against all people they consider heretics or infidels that it has been disowned by Al-Qaida's leaders.

The President said in a speech in North Carolina this morning at Duke University that, "America does not forget" and vowed justice for harm done to any kidnapped American.

We were all sobered upon reading the news release. And, at least it gave us some further information to consider.

The Ambassador then continued his briefing to us.

"Nothing official has been established, but our GPS on the kidnap vehicle shows that they abandoned it at one of the beaches heading out of Tel Aviv towards Jerusalem," said the Ambassador. "And that was their first big mistake."

"So, you have the car?" Bill asked.

"Yes, we do, and there was some blood in the car; we believe it was from the initial fight at the hotel and not from Liz, since she is valuable to both sides. However, blood samples are undergoing analysis even as we speak," he added.

He went on to explain that they did not yet know what the transfer vehicle was or how many people were in it.

"Yet?" asked Bill.

"Yes," replied the ambassador. "Israeli drones were sent up in the air right away. They picked up the GPS signal immediately. Because of that, they began tracking the highway and roads leading into Palestinian controlled territory from where the government vehicle was abandoned. By eliminating the cars that left the road before Egypt, the drones were able to narrow things down to just a few suspect vehicles. We are now waiting for their tracking report."

"So, what you are actually saying is that you have no idea where my wife is or who has her or where they have her or…," Bill lashed out, angrily.

A moment later, Bill's cell phone rang. He picked it up and there was a man with an Arabic accent on the other end.

"Mr. Stein," he shouted, "The Islamic State of Palestine has your wife and we want to negotiate with the American government for her release."

"Is she okay, is she okay? Let me speak with Liz!" Bill shouted back into the phone as the room went silent.

Agent James just motioned to Bill to keep him talking, while Tim and Sam raced out and then quickly brought in a cart of tech equipment into the room.

"First things first…" said the voice on the phone.

"Let me speak to my wife, you snake! That is the first thing," Bill shouted.

"I won't allow that, but you can look at YouTube clip, which is now online.

The agents found it almost immediately. It was very brief.

"Bill, I am okay, we drove for hours… I love you," Liz exclaimed in a scared voice.

Then the man came back on the phone and told Bill that Liz would stay safe as long as negotiations were going well.

"I give you one hour to arrange meeting, then I call you back," the man ordered Bill. And with that he ended the call.

Bill was visibly shaken. Although, the agents said he had

done a good job. However, he wasn't on long enough for them to find where the signal was coming from. It was smart of them to use a YouTube clip rather than dwelling on the phone. Despite all that, Liz had given us a clue – whether intentionally or not, we did not know. She said that they had driven for hours. The bad guy said that she was taken by The Islamic State of Palestine or ISP. When they put those two facts together, the three agents concluded that she was most likely being held in one of their secret prisons in Gaza, probably at the prison called Al Azali, because it was closest to the border and in the northern Sinai Peninsula, which was once a Hamas stronghold but now under the control of ISP. The three agents assigned to us – James, Tim, and Sam – seemed to be quite informed and this was reassuring, especially to Bill. By now, he and I were guessing that this trio of agents were all CIA. James, the lead agent, told us that according to Amnesty International, prisoners released from this prison estimated that several hundred political prisoners were being held there, mostly awaiting trial.

"Do they torture people there?" Bill bravely asked.

"I am not going to sugarcoat it," said James. "The reports tell of people being hung from their hands or their feet and those who scream out are hit. The cells are over-crowded, no electricity, two-minute timed bathroom breaks only once a day. Meals are soup with bread and water, once a day."

"Officially, these secret places do not exist so there is no judicial oversight of them," said Tim. "Consequently, no one from the Palestinian government authority knows anything about these prisoners, at least on the record."

"It's a bad situation for sure," said James.

"However, the silver lining is that we think we know where she is being held and we also know that they do not want to harm or kill her, because of the ransom demands," added agent Sam.

"That's right," said Tim. "And they are likely keeping her in a special private cell, away from the other prisoners."

At this point, Elaine just lost it and broke down crying.

"I am so sorry Bill," she said. "I need to tell you Al's dying words.

"Dying words? ...Al's gone?" Bill snapped back.

"Yes, I did not know quite when to share it, but he died in my arms at the scene in front of the hotel." He said to tell you, "If it weren't for me, Liz would never would have gotten into this mess.

So, please forgive me."

Bill just hugged Elaine, and told her that's not true.

"It's not Al's fault. It's not Al's fault," Bill kept repeating, as he too sobbed openly. I guess we all were beginning to come apart, at this point in the ordeal.

Ambassador Kaplan had heard about Al's bravery in trying to save Liz. He assured us that he would make arrangements to send flowers on our behalf, to Al's funeral, whenever and wherever it was held. Israeli agents Nate and Mike also assured us, on behalf of the Prime Minister, that Al would receive a proper burial at the proper time and that his dual citizenship and Christian faith would be respected and acknowledged. It was clear that we would probably not be able to attend our dear friend's funeral, so that was a very thoughtful gesture, especially under these circumstances.

"Look," said agent James. "They said they would be calling back in an hour; we need to be prepared for that call."

It didn't take long. Just about an hour from the first call, the second call came in to Bill's phone. This time the kidnappers wanted to speak to American officials, not Bill, so Agent James took the phone. The kidnappers demanded the release of fifty specific

Palestinian prisoners reported to be held in France, Germany, Guantanamo Bay, and Israel.

In addition, they wanted ten million American dollars and a promise from Israel that it would abandon plans to build a new Temple on the old Temple site. They threatened to kill Liz if their demands were not met in three days. Quickly, and to gain more time, the US and Israeli governments opened secret negotiations with ISP. From the drone information and intelligence gathered from previously released prisoners, Mossad drew up a rescue plan during the night.

The following day a rescue mission called Lightning Bolt was approved by the Prime Minister of Israel, with the full knowledge and approval of the United States President. From there, things moved quite expeditiously.

CHAPTER 26

CRISIS RESOLUTION

We only learned after its conclusion, that under the complete cover of darkness and in the pre-dawn hours of the next night, an Israeli C-130 transport and three black hawk helicopters approached the small town in Gaza near where the prison was located. It carried two dozen Israeli commandos, a Mercedes, and two military transport vehicles. A few of the commandos were dressed in police uniforms. The Mercedes was made to resemble an official looking military car and the other vehicles were made to look like official police vehicles, with all the proper flags and signage. And the plan worked; at least they were not discovered until they reached the front entrance of the small prison. At the moment of detection by the guards at the front gate, the Israelis stormed the building, freeing as many prisoners as they could, killing as many terrorists as they could, and withdrawing with Liz safe in hand. As they withdrew the Israelis destroyed all the cars nearby, in order to prevent pursuit back to the plane. The entire rescue operation had taken roughly ninety minutes from landing to take off.

Once airborne, the Israelis flew to Tel Aviv. There was a complete medical team on the plane, including a psychiatrist. After landing, Liz was transferred to a Mossad vehicle and taken directly to their headquarters inside a government compound.

In all, the raid freed an estimated one hundred political prisoners. In the fighting, six prisoners were killed, as well as roughly two dozen terrorists. Unfortunately, two Israeli commandos were also killed. They were the ones who actually reached the basement room where Liz was being held. They were hit by several hand grenades before backup arrived on the scene. There were also several wounded Israeli commandos.

A full medical emergency unit had been set up in the compound, so Liz was immediately checked out again more fully by medical personnel, including a team of psychiatrists. Only after all of that was she allowed to call Bill, briefly. It would take the next two days for formal debriefing by Mossad, and our State Department. That debriefing was led by agents James, Tim and Sam. It was this trio that broke the news to her about Al Hoffman's heroics and his passing.

On the morning of the third day they drove Liz back to the American Embassy, where we all reunited. Thoughtfully, everyone allowed the four of us to be by ourselves through lunch and for the afternoon. Actually, Liz and Bill retired to their room shortly after lunch, but not until she had made a startling announcement.

"I did it while I was so scared of dying in that prison," Liz said.

"What did you do?" asked Bill.

"I made the decision to put faith in Jesus Christ as my Messiah and I used the sinner's prayer that Al made me promise to memorize," Liz explained.

While Elaine and I were quietly rejoicing over Liz's commitment to Christ, we tried to stay very sensitive to both of our friends during the traumatic experience they were going through. We did not see them until the next morning. During breakfast, Bill and Liz informed us that they had made some crucial decisions. Liz was more resolved than ever to live in Israel and work on the Temple re-building project. They were going to approach Pam, the realtor, and try to work out taking over Al's lease on his condo. As Liz said,

"He does not need it, since he is enjoying a mansion in heaven and an eternity with Christ, or I guess I should say, Yeshua."

"And knowing Al," said Elaine, "he would be thrilled to know that you are taking it over and continuing on with the project."

"Yes, and it is also near Al's church, which is where I hope to begin worshipping as soon as possible," said Liz.

"That all sounds great," I said.

"But what about you, Bill, what are your thoughts on all of this?"

"That's the tough part. I don't know if I can adjust to a new life here, given all the drama, trauma, the spiritual change for Liz, and prospects for more danger lurking ahead. I just am going to need some time to process it all. So, I am going back to Lexington for a while," said a down-trodden Bill Stein.

Breakfast became very, very quiet at that point. The emotional anguish our friend was going through was almost palpable to us.

The three of us left for home a couple of days later on a plane supplied by the US State Department, while Liz remained behind to start therapy and her new life in her new country, with her new faith.

183

THE END

Afterword

My name is Dan Moretti, Joe and Elaine's son, a sociologist by training and heretofore an agnostic, despite my Christian upbringing. I am writing this afterword to my father's account of my mom's and his interactions with the Steins during their planned move to Israel several years ago. If you have read my father's rendition of events, you already know that they tried to warn their valued friends of what their church taught them about end-time events in Israel and the Middle East prior to the second coming of Jesus Christ. As a sociologist, I had long ago forsaken the biblical teachings of my parents. Growing up, I gave lip service to it intellectually, but never put my full trust in Christ as my Lord and Savior. I was too intelligent, well-educated, modern and sophisticated for religion, or so I told myself.

My pride in myself and my abilities and my desire to run my own life had kept me from truly considering the facts about Christ and from putting my trust in Him for my salvation. However, I have now been shaken to my core by the fact that my mom and dad are gone. They were taken in an instant, along with millions of others around the world. It took place several weeks ago during a worldwide series of catastrophic events: earthquakes, tsunamis, raging fires, one event seemingly triggering another and stretching around the globe. Then on top of all that, authorities were beginning to report about planes crashing, trains going off their tracks, massive car accidents, big rig trucks causing highway pile ups, ships run aground, and so forth. The one thing they all seem to have in common is that more often than not, the people driving, navigating, or piloting could not be found, dead or alive. The same was also true for many of their passengers, young and old, alike. Along with all of this calamity, as one might imagine, came mass panic and confusion. Power and communications were out everywhere, which in turn led to riots and looting. Later, I remember thinking what a miracle it was that The 1948 Store, though looted and damaged, still stood.

However, clearly and more importantly, what some call the global infrastructure was in shambles. And to this day sociologists, scientists, military people and other experts have yet to agree as to what really caused it all to take place. Of course, with my Christian upbringing, I knew in my unbelieving heart of hearts what it was.

For it could only logically be one thing, God's taking away or rapture of His church - the invisible church of all true Christian believers, like my mom and dad. I also quickly came to realize that since the rapture had now taken place, the time remaining until the world attacked Israel and the culminating battle of Armageddon took place was now only a few short years away. Funny, the things you also recall at a time like this, not that there has ever been another truly comparable time like this one. I remember reading a poem by Clive Cussler, the noted author of a number of great books. The poem, although short, is still very meaningful. It goes something like this.

Topsy-turvy,
Turvy-topsy,
The world stands on its head,
The sky's on fire,
The earth's afraid.
The ocean leaves its bed.
6. Citations

After a day of panic, fear, and searching for mom and dad, the total reality of the rapture sank deeply into my soul, and by God's grace I turned in faith, to Jesus Christ as my Lord and Savior. I prayed for Him to forgive me of my sins and unbelief and to have mercy on my soul. My heart was immediately warmed by God's assuring love and acceptance of me, a prodigal, into His family.

With my new faith comes a different point of view. So, I now also can fully appreciate and understand what my Mom and Dad believed about end-times events. I found this from a dear Christian brother of my parents, Rodney Jim Forest. Rodney had a tough job before the rapture. He was a police officer in Houston, Texas, or to be more precise, a Texas Ranger. Rodney also had a tender heart towards Christ and towards people. Here is his inspired poem.

On The Sands of Time

In the valley the sky grows dim
As the world turns from Him
The buzzards gather in the East
Circling around their precious feast

The pieces moving into place
As he prepares to show his face
America bending at the knee
Has she fulfilled her destiny?

Once a haven for truth and right
Now politicians restrain her might
Evil is called good and good they despise
This is happening right before our eyes

The man of sin is alive and well
Is this the time, who can tell?
Christians purged and hated
The Word of God is desecrated

Yet soon the trumpet will surely sound
Not one believer will be found
As the final sand runs from the glass

From this earth the spirit will pass

Soon judgment will fall upon the earth
Like a woman giving birth
When this time has begun
Fear not, the victory has been won

The horse is saddled for the fight
When Jesus comes and sets things right
Trust The Lord with all your heart
From the faith never depart

7. Citations

As wonderful as that moment was, I very soon realized that the rest of my days on earth were going to be spent during very perilous times, since Christ's followers were no longer on Earth, helping to restrain evil and knowing that the antichrist would now soon be revealed to begin his oppression. Then, he would soon be gathering an army to move against Israel. So, it is really now a full-tilt dire march to Armageddon for all of us that remain on earth.

In searching through Mom and Dad's home, I found his account of his time with Liz and Bill Stein. He titled it *1948*. So, one of things that I have decided to do is to finish his work and to try to get it out to as many people as possible. Lord only knows, the world remains in a state of shock and fear. Most people certainly have no real clue as to what actually took place and the implications for our lives going forward.

I was at The 1948 Store one day with Hugo, who also has made a faith commitment to Christ. During the rapture, the store windows had been shattered from a car going through them. The driver must have been a believer, because he or she was not to be found. However, all in all, the store was intact. After phone service was finally restored, we noticed a message had been placed on our answering machine. I called the number back and after several tries, reached Dr. Bill Stein, who was still living nearby in Boston. Unfortunately, he and Liz divorced only a year after he returned home from their trip to Israel with my parents.

"Hi, Dr. Stein. This is Dan Moretti, Joe and Elaine's son. Thank God you are alright," I began.

"Dan, I am shaken to the core. I am alive, but not really alright. How's your mom and dad, are they...are they...?" Bill's voice trailed off.

"Yes, they are gone. Only the prodigal in the family, me, is left," I replied.

"So all that about the rapture is true, it's true! That is what must have happened to Liz, too." He rambled on a bit.

"Yes, it's all true," I interjected "Our government is trying to blame it on some alien invasion from outer space, but most aren't buying it."

"Oh well, I guess that makes as much sense to me, after the 'rapture' or whatever the heck it was that took place, as the Israeli government's official explanation. The authorities there are trying to claim that it was some kind of mysterious 'perfect storm' of hundreds of meteors hitting earth, while Islamic terrorists kidnapped millions of hostages, simultaneously targeting Christians worldwide in a massive Jihad surprise attack. I don't think even the government buys it, I sure don't." Bill said adamantly. Then he continued rambling more.

"My Christian friend, Howie King from Cranston, Rhode Island, was keeping me up-to-date. He received a lot of messages by ham radio from Israel. Howie finally got me into ham radio about a year ago, so I could also keep up with unfolding events in the Middle East for myself. It's a good thing too, because Howie is now missing as well."

Bill then went on to share further, that although divorced, Liz and he had remained friends and communicated regularly. She told him a short time before the rapture that the re-building of the Temple was going quite well.

"Well what are you doing? Are you safe, eating, working? Look, Hugo and I are still nearby here in Boston, so whatever we can do to help, please let us know. We are still trying to get the store back to normal, whatever normal is now. I guess it's really another 'new normal,' like after 9/11. However, what is new for sure, is that Hugo and I have both accepted Christ as our Savior, as have my wife, Jann and our two kids, Linda and Lisa," I told him.

Bill basically ignored my announcement and replied, "I see."

Then abruptly re-focusing the discussion, Bill went on to say, "Oh if there is anything to be thankful for, I guess it's that my house was not damaged. And from what I gather, the Temple site, so precious to Liz, was not touched at all. I'm just trying to do as much as I can to deal with it all personally, and I'm doing a lot of hospital volunteering since this all happened. It's the least I can do, to help our community."

"The obvious questions is, Dr. Stein, what will you do regarding faith in Jesus Christ?" I challenged him.

"I see things more from your Christian faith perspective

now, but my mind is still wrestling it through. I guess you could say, I am almost persuaded," Bill said emotionally.

We chatted a bit more and he assured me he had my mom's notebook and the Bible Al had given him. Unfortunately, in the post-rapture "normal" world, communications, including phones and the internet, were now increasingly inoperative or restricted to business and emergency calls only. That conversation took place well over a year ago now. We have never communicated with Bill again after that day on the phone.

APPENDIX A: ELAINE'S NOTEBOOK

REFERS TO CHAPTER 10

Based in part on *God's Prophetic Calendar, Beyond Beliefs to Convictions* and the Bible.

Elaine's notebook was comprised of the following items:

ITEM 1: Twenty established fact about the life of Christ while he was on earth, as accurately predicted some 400 years prior to his birth.

The predictions can be found in the Psalms, Isaiah, Zechariah and other places in the Old Testament. They are listed below.

1. He will be born in Bethlehem

2. He will be a descendant of King David

3. He will be betrayed by a friend

4. The price of his betrayal will be 30 pieces of silver

5. He will be deserted by his disciples

6. He will ride into the city of Jerusalem on a donkey

7. He will be silent before his accusers

8. He will be wounded and bruised

9. He will be hated without a cause

10. He will be mocked, ridiculed and rejected

11. He will collapse from weakness

12. He will be executed among sinners

13. His hands and feet will be pierced

14. He will pray for his persecutors

15. He will thirst, but only be given gall and vinegar

16. His bones will be left unbroken, but his heart will rupture

17. His side will be pierced

18. Darkness will be over the land at midday

19. He will be buried in a rich man's tomb

20. He will be raised from the dead on the third day after his death

ITEM 2: Christ demonstrated his godly supernatural power over the body, gravity, weather and death through the following recorded miracles which he performed in front of many, both believers and skeptics, while on earth.

Calmed a storm

Made a mute person speak

Fed five thousand people with five loaves and two fish

Cast out demons

Walked on water

Brought sight to the blind

Healed a paralyzed man

Foretold the future

Raised a boy from the dead

Cleansed lepers

Turned water into wine

Made the lame walk

Forgave sin

Raised a man from the dead

ITEM 3: Christ appeared to ten different people or groups after he was resurrected from the dead.

1. Mary of Magdala

2. The women returning from the tomb

3. Peter

4. Two followers on the road to Emmaus

5. The disciples and a number of others

6. The disciples including doubting Thomas

7. Seven disciples by the Sea of Galilee

8. A crowd of followers of more than 500

9. His human brother, James

10. The eleven disciples at His ascension

NOTE: The above list from the Bible was compiled by author Josh McDowell and recorded in his book, *Beyond Beliefs to Convictions*, pages 65, 76 and 272, respectively

"What extraordinary lengths God went to in order to help people identify and recognize his only begotten Son!" Josh McDowell said.

Professor Peter W. Stoner, in an analysis that was carefully reviewed and pronounced to be sound by the American Scientific Affiliation, states that the probability of just eight of these prophecies being fulfilled in one person is 1 in 10 trillion. (page 67, *Beyond Beliefs to Convictions*)

ITEM 4: A prophetic checklist for the nations

☐ The establishment of the United Nations begins a serious first step toward world government.

☐ The rebuilding of Europe after WW II makes possible its future role in a renewal of the Roman Empire.

☐ Israel is reestablished as a nation.

☐ Russia rises to be a world power and then becomes the ally of Arab countries.

☐ The Common Market and World Bank are established because of a need for some international regulation of the world economy.

☐ Red China rises to be a world power and develops the capacity to field an army of 200,000,000, as predicted in prophecy.

☐ The Middle East becomes the most significant trouble spot in the world.

☐ The oil blackmail awakens the world to the new concentration of wealth and power in the Mediterranean.

☐ The Iron Curtain falls and a new order emerges in Europe.

- Russia declines as a world power and loses her influence in the Middle East.

- A world clamoring for peace follows the continued disruption caused in the high price of oil, terrorist incidents, and the confused military situation in the Middle East.

- Ten nations create a united Mediterranean Confederacy; beginning the last stage of the prophetic fourth world empire.

- In a dramatic power play, a new Mediterranean leader upsets three nations of the confederacy and takes control of the powerful ten-nation group.

- The new Mediterranean leader negotiates a "final" peace settlement in the Middle East (broken three and a half years later).

- The Russian army attempts an invasion of Israel and is miraculously destroyed, mostly by catastrophic weather events.

- The Mediterranean leader proclaims himself world dictator, breaks his peace settlement with Israel and declares himself to be God.

- The new world dictator desecrates the temple in Jerusalem.

☐ The terrible judgments of the Great Tribulation are poured out on the nations of the world.

☐ Worldwide rebellion threatens the world dictator's rule as armies from throughout the world converge on the Middle East.

☐ Christ returns to earth with His armies from heaven.

☐ The armies of the world unite to resist Christ's coming and are destroyed in the Battle of Armageddon.

☐ Christ establishes His millennial reign on earth, ending the times of the Gentiles.

ITEM 5: A prophetic checklist for Israel.

☐ The intense suffering and persecution of Jews throughout the world leads to pressure for a national home in Palestine.

☐ Jews return to Palestine, and Israel is reestablished as a nation in 1948.

☐ The infant nation survives against overwhelming odds.

☐ Russia emerges as an important enemy of Israel, but the United States comes to the aid of Israel.

☐ Israel's heroic survival and growing strength makes it an

established nation, recognized throughout the world.

- ☐ Israel's military accomplishments become overshadowed by the Arabs' ability to wage a diplomatic war by controlling much of the world's oil reserves.

- ☐ The Arab position is strengthened by their growing wealth and by alliances between Europe and key Arab countries.

- ☐ The increasing isolation of the United States and Russia from the Middle East makes it more and more difficult for Israel to negotiate an acceptable peace settlement.

- ☐ After a long struggle, Israel is forced to accept a compromise peace guaranteed by the new leader of the Mediterranean Confederacy of ten nations.

- ☐ The Jewish people celebrate what appears to be a lasting and final peace settlement.

- ☐ During three-and-a-half years of peace, Judaism is revived, and traditional sacrifices and ceremonies are re-instituted in the rebuilt temple in Jerusalem.

- ☐ The Russian army attempts to invade Israel but is mysteriously destroyed, mostly by catastrophic weather events.

- [ ] The newly proclaimed world dictator desecrates the temple in Jerusalem and begins a period of intense persecution of Jews.

- [ ] Many Jews recognize the unfolding of prophetic events and declare their faith in Christ as the Messiah of Israel.

- [ ] In the massacre of Jews and Christians who resist the world dictator, some witnesses are divinely preserved to carry the message throughout the world. They number 144,000.

- [ ] Christ returns to earth, welcomed by believing Jews as their Messiah.

- [ ] Christ's thousand-year reign on earth from the throne of David finally fulfills the prophetic promises to the Jewish people.

ITEM 6: A prophetic check list for the church.

- [ ] The rise of world Communism in the 20th century makes possible the worldwide spread of atheism.

- [ ] Liberalism undermines the spiritual vitality of the church in Europe and eventually America.

- [ ] The movement toward a super-church begins with the

ecumenical movement.

- Apostasy and open denial of biblical truth is evident in the church.

- Moral chaos becomes more and more evident because of the complete departure from Christian morality.

- The sweep of the occult, and belief in demons begins to prepare the world for Satan's final hour.

- Jerusalem becomes a center of religious controversy for Arabs and Christians, while Jews of the world plan to make the city an active center for Judaism.

- True believers disappear from the earth to join Christ in heaven at the Rapture of the church.

- The restraint of evil by the Holy Spirit ends.

- The super-church combines major religions as a tool for the False Prophet who aids the Antichrist's rise to world power.

- The Antichrist destroys the super-church and demands worship as a deified world dictator.

- Believers of this period suffer intense persecution and are martyred by the thousands.

- Christ returns to the earth with Christians who have been in heaven during the Tribulation and ends the rule of the nations at the battle of Armageddon.

ITEM 7: Prophetic events in history, beginning with the Babylonian Captivity.

605 B.C. Fall of Jerusalem: beginning of Babylonian Captivity and the Times of the Gentiles

586 B.C. Destruction of Jerusalem and Solomon's temple

539 B.C. Fall of Babylon: beginning of second empire of Medo-Persia

538 B.C. Second return of the Jews to the Holy Land

515 B.C. Rebuilding of Temple in Jerusalem

445 B.C. Rebuilding of Jerusalem Walls

445-396 B.C. City of Jerusalem rebuilt

331 B.C. The third empire of Greece

242 B.C. The fourth empire of Rome

63 B.C. Romans conquer Jerusalem

20 B.C. Romans begin rebuilding of Jerusalem temple.

6 B.C. Birth of Jesus Christ

A.D. 30-33 Ministry, death and resurrection of Jesus Christ

A.D. 64 Jerusalem Temple completed

A.D. 70 Destruction of Jerusalem and Temple: worldwide scattering of the Jews

A.D. 1897 Zionist movement begins: Israel seeks home in ancient land

A.D. 1945 Rise of Russia and Communism to power

A.D. 1946 Beginning of world government: United Nations formed

A.D. 1948 Israel established as a nation in the land: third return

A.D. 1948 Beginning of world church: formation of the World Council of Churches

Based on the Bible, and lists compiled by John F. Walvoord in his book, *Armageddon, Oil and the Middle East Crises*, pp. 107-108; 219-224.

ITEM 8: Some key Bible verses pointing to Christ's second coming

"The Son of Man shall come in the glory of his Father with his angels, and then shall he reward every man according to his works."

Matthew 16:27

"Hereinafter shall ye see the Son of Man sitting on the right hand of power, and coming in the clouds of heaven with power and great glory...but of that day and hour knoweth no man...watch therefore...Be ready; for in such an hour as ye think not the Son of Man cometh. ... Two women shall be ... together; one shall be taken and the other left. Two men shall be in the field, one shall be taken and the other left. ... There shall be signs in the sun, and moon and stars and on the earth, distress of nations...men's hearts failing them for fear and expectation of the things that are coming on the earth, for the powers of heaven shall be shaken. And then shall they see the Son of Man coming in a cloud with power and great glory. And when these things begin to come to pass, look up and lift up your heads, for your redemption draweth nigh." Matthew 24

"In the last days there shall be scoffers, saying where is the promise of His coming...Beloved, be not ignorant of this one thing, that one day is with the Lord as a thousand years...

"The Lord is not slack concerning His promise...

"The day of the Lord will come...in which the heavens shall pass away with a great noise, and the elements shall melt and fervent heat and the earth and the works therein shall be burned up...

"But according to His promise, we look for New Heavens and a New Earth." Peter 3

"Christ was once offered to bear the sins of many and to them that look for him he shall appear the second time, apart from sin, unto salvation." Hebrews 9:28

"In my Father's house are many mansions; if it were not so, I would have told you. I go to prepare a place for you. And if I go and prepare a place for you, I will come again and receive you unto myself, that where I am, there ye may be also." John 14:3

ITEM 9: Dr. Billy Graham's crusade commitment prayer.

"I have led tens of thousands who have come forward to make decisions for Christ in every part of the world in this simple prayer: O God, I am a sinner, I'm sorry for my sins. I'm willing to turn from my sins. I receive Christ as Savior. I confess Him as Lord. From this moment on I want to follow Him and serve Him in the fellowship of His church. In Christ's name, Amen." (Graham 308)

APPENDIX B: AL'S RESURRECTION EVIDENCE NOTEBOOK

REFERS TO CHAPTER 21

Evidence: Inspired by the writings of the Bible, Frank Morrison, and other. However, all quotes are by Frank Morrison in his book, *Who Moved the Stone?*

POINT ONE: The tomb was empty.

Refutation:

"It is impossible to read the records of the period without being profoundly impressed by the way in which, for friend and foe alike, the tomb of Jesus sinks into utter and undisturbed oblivion. No one in later years seems to have gone to Joseph's garden, and looking at the rock-hewn cave, to have said, 'This is the place the Lord is buried.' No hostile investigations seem to have been made to show that the martyred remains of the great Teacher sill lay where they were deposited some days, weeks, or months earlier. Still more strikingly, no one pretending to have an intimate and special knowledge seems to have said, 'Not here was He ultimately buried, but there.' Instead of these quite natural consequences flowing from so extraordinary an event, we get the stony appearance of indifference. From the moment the women returned from the Garden, the tomb of Jesus passed, historically, into complete oblivion...The assumption that the tomb was empty seems to have been universal. The only controversy of which we have any record, and it was clearly a heated one, was on the vexed question as to whether the disciples had secretly removed the body. This, I say, is a very formidable fact. It suggests that something had already occurred to make the vacancy of the tomb common ground, and to place it high out of the reach of dispute or argument." (Morrison 111-12)

POINT TWO: The disciples stole the body.

Refutation:

"...where anybody could go and see the tomb...and where an overwhelming body of official, authoritative and conclusive witness existed. Yet, it is in this center of solid...realism that, according to Luke, no fewer than three thousand converts were made...increased shortly afterward to five thousand. What was the determining factor in this steady erosion into the Judean body that in a few short years

209

became so serious and widespread that Saul of Tarsus was driven to organize a tremendous campaign of suppression against it? Whence came the drive that convinced one reasonable person after another that the Christians were right and the priests were wrong? Could anything have prospered with the disciples if...the tomb itself had given a silent and impenetrable no!

"...it was repugnant and out of keeping with their known moral qualities and their singularly unimaginative type of mind." page 114

"We have to account not merely for the enthusiasm of its friends, but for the paralysis of its enemies and for the ever-growing stream of new converts that came over to it. When we remember what certain highly placed personages in Jerusalem would almost certainly have given to have strangled this movement at its birth but could not." (Morrison 115)

POINT THREE: His enemies stole the body.

Refutation:

"We realize also why it was that throughout the four years when Christianity was growing to really formidable dimensions in Jerusalem, neither Caiaphas, nor Annas, nor any recognized

210

member of the Sadducean Camarilla, whose prestige and personal repute was so deeply affronted and outraged by the new doctrine, ever took the obvious shortcut out of their difficulties. If the body of Jesus still lay in the tomb...why did they not say so? A cold and dispassionate statement of the real facts, issued by someone in authority, and publicly exhibited in the temple precincts, would have been like a bucket of water upon the kindling fire of Christian heresy." (Morrison116)

GENERAL SUMMATION:

"When we remember the swinging around of the disciples from panic fear to absolute certitude ... the extraordinarily rapid adhesion of converts in Jerusalem, the strange absence of administrative vigor on the part of authorities, the steady growing of the church, both in authority and power ...we realize that we are in the presence of something far more tangible than the psychological repercussion of a fisherman's dream."

APPENDIX C: LIZ'S NOTES FOR THE TEMPLE.

REFERS TO CHAPTER 18

- The original Temple was 90' long and 45' wide and 3 stories high.

- Solomon built first Temple, which Babylonians destroyed in 586 B.C.

- In 20 B.C., Herod started building the second temple. It took 80 years to complete.

- Romans destroyed it 10 years later in A.D. 70, along with destroying all of Jerusalem.

- Never been rebuilt in over 2000 years.

- Temple site so holy that all preparation work on the stone foundation and walls was done away from the site.

- No tools, such as hammers, awls or iron tools of any kind were ever used at the site, so that not even the sounds of construction would desecrate the site.

- The Ark of the Covenant: Israel's most holy object. Made of acacia wood,   overlaid with gold, very ornate. Was considered God's footstool or throne on the earth. Contained Ten Commandments, a pot of manna and Aaron's rod. The

Ark's dimensions formed a perfect cube. Destroyed by the Babylonians in 586 B.C.

- Innermost room was the Holy of Holies and it is where the Ark of Covenant was kept.

- 7 branched lampstand for light (known as the menorah)

- Worship at the Temple was often very messy, because so much had to do with killing sacrificial lambs.

- The sacrificial altars had channels on their sides for carrying away all the blood.

- The Mikveh bath was the place for ritualistic washings.

- Herod greatly expanded the Temple that Jesus knew. It had a number of courtyards, chambers, and gates. This is the Temple Jesus predicted would be destroyed and it was in A.D. 70.

- The outer courtyard of the Temple was known as the court of the gentiles. No gentiles could go beyond this point – on punishment of death.

- Temple hill was sloped on all sides.

- Temple Mount measured 300 meters by 500 meters and the

height of the walls reached as high as 50 meters.

- Solomon's Temple was built with much gold (plentiful at the time), stone blocks, cedar, olive, and cypress trees, metals, including gold, silver, bronze and iron, fabric of purple, violet and crimson and precious stones.

- Altars must have small platforms for seating of Rabbis. They taught sitting down and read scrolls of scripture standing up, out of respect for the scripture.

APPENDIX D: AL'S MESSIANIC CHURCH.

REFERENCE TO CHAPTER 17

(Adapted mainly from Rochester, NY Messianic Church

Informational Website)

- Welcome to Congregation Shemar Y'Israel! We are a Messianic Jewish congregation, a community of about 125 Jewish and non-Jewish people of diverse backgrounds worshiping and serving the G-d of Abraham, Isaac and Jacob. We also follow his son, Yeshua (commonly called Jesus) the Messiah, as described in Isaiah, chapter 53.
- We follow Biblical Judaism, rather than rabbinical Judaism, and teach both the Old and New Covenants from a Jewish perspective. We follow G-d's Law and his Spirit as we seek to deepen our relationship with him, grow more like him and live out his nature in our daily lives. Our desire is to live out G-d's purpose for the Jewish people as a "light to the world" while living out his plan for our individual lives. We want to help others do the same. We also seek to advance G-d's spiritual Kingdom of love, truth, justice and mercy on earth.
- Committed to restoring the Jewish roots of our faith, we celebrate the Jewish holidays and worship G-d through the prayers of our Fathers in Hebrew and English. We also love to worship through songs sung in Hebrew and English and though a Davidic-style of Israeli folk dance. We are a place where Jewish people can worship the G-d of Israel and follow Yeshua as the Messiah while keeping their Jewish identity.
- At the same time, we welcome non-Jewish people who want to come alongside the Jewish people to worship G-d in a Jewish way, as the Moabite Ruth in the Bible left her homeland to join herself to Israel. We believe that Yeshua's death and resurrection broke down the wall of animosity and division between Jew and Gentile so we can live and worship in unity.

- Congregation Israel, is just one of many Messianic Jewish congregations around the world. There is at least one congregation in most major cities in the United States and more than 100 congregations in Israel. There are also many congregations in Canada, Europe, Latin and South America, Africa, Asia and Australia. G-d's Spirit is moving among the Jewish people in a new way, showing them how they can have faith in Yeshua and still be Jewish.

ACKNOWLEGEMENTS

(in no particular order)

The Johnsons of the Caribbean for hosting the author during his final draft review

Deborah Croizier, Chief of Proof Reading

Douglas Antocicco, Chief of Technical Support

Daniel Antocicco, Technical Support

David Antocicco, Cover Design

Lois Sorensen, Proof Reading

Maria Bradeen, Proof Reading

Michele Antocicco, Technical Support

The Webster Public Library very able and helpful staff, Webster, NY

Citations

1. Graham, Billy. *Storm Warnings.* Thomas Nelson Publishing. 1992. p 287

2. Orwell, George. *1984.* Signet Books Publishing. 1961. Fromm, Eric, Afterword.

3. Blood Moon topics were inspired by the various sermons and writings of Rev. John Hagee and others.

4. Rochester, NY. Messianic Church Website

5. Morrison, Frank. *Who Moved The Stone?* Zondervan Publishing. 1987.

6. Cussler, Clive, Poem Author 1. *Polar Shift*

7. Sellers, Rodney, Poem Author 2. Baytown, Texas

8. Griswold, Millie, Editor. *God's Prophetic Calendar.* Advent General Conference Publishing. 1983

9. Walvoord, John F. *Armegeddon, Oil and the Middle East Crisis.* Zondervan Publishing. 1990.

10. McDowell, Josh, Hostetler, Bob. *Beyond Belief to Convictions.* Tyndale Publishing. 2002.

11. Holy Bible, various translations and sections.

39357772R00140

Made in the USA
Charleston, SC
05 March 2015